D1459041

Dan Lee spends his time travelling between Asia and Britain. A wing chun master, he also trains in kickboxing and ju-jitsu.

Books in The Tangshan Tigers series

TANGSHAN TIGERS

The Stolen Jade

Dan Lee

PUFFIN

For James and Deborah Noble

With special thanks to Brandon Robshaw

PUFFIN BOOKS

Published by the Penguin Group
Penguin Books Ltd, 80 Strand, London WC2R 0RL, England
Penguin Group (USA) Inc., 375 Hudson Street, New York, New York 10014, USA
Penguin Group (Canada), 90 Eglinton Avenue East, Suite 700, Toronto, Ontario, Canada M4P 2Y3
(a division of Pearson Penguin Canada Inc.)
Penguin Ireland, 25 St Stephen's Green, Dublin 2, Ireland (a division of Penguin Books Ltd)
Penguin Group (Australia), 250 Camberwell Road, Camberwell, Victoria 3124, Australia
(a division of Pearson Australia Group Pty Ltd)
Penguin Books India Pvt Ltd, 11 Community Centre, Panchsheel Park,
New Delhi – 110 017, India
Penguin Group (NZ), 67 Apollo Drive, Rosedale, North Shore 0632, New Zealand
(a division of Pearson New Zealand Ltd)
Penguin Books (South Africa) (Pty) Ltd, 24 Sturdee Avenue, Rosebank,
Johannesburg 2196, South Africa

Penguin Books Ltd, Registered Offices: 80 Strand, London WC2R 0RL, England

puffinbooks.co.uk

Published 2008
1

Series created by Working Partners, London
Text copyright © Working Partners Ltd, 2008

Typese

Except in
that it shall
circulated v
than that in v

A Cl

CONTENTS

THE FIRST DAY

'Wow!' said Matt.

'Yes,' smiled his mother. 'Impressive, isn't it?'

The pale morning sun shone on the vast red and gold building that was the Beijing International Academy.

'It looks like a temple or something!' said Matt.

'Traditional Chinese architecture, in the style of the Han Dynasty,' his mother told him, slamming the car door shut behind her. 'But you'll find it's pretty modern inside.'

Matt hardly heard his mother's words, his

excitement growing as they climbed up the wide, imposing steps. Wind-chimes tinkled as the doors parted before them.

They found themselves in a large entrance hall with a dizzyingly high ceiling. A fountain burbled. On the wall, a huge plasma screen read WELCOME TO THE BEIJING INTERNATIONAL ACADEMY, with a constantly changing visual display beneath. There were scores of boys and girls milling about, and Matt could see at a glance why this was called the *International* Academy – some looked European, some looked Asian, some American, some African . . . It reminded him of an embassy party he'd once been to with his mother, only this time with kids instead of grown-ups.

As he walked across the foyer, a few kids turned round and stared. Feeling self-conscious, Matt smiled. One boy, a stocky, dark-haired kid with glasses, about Matt's age, smiled back.

Matt's mother approached the reception desk where a smartly dressed Chinese man with a tiny black beard stood, waiting politely. She said something in rapid Mandarin. The receptionist bowed and replied in perfect English: 'Ah yes, Ambassador James, we have been expecting you – you were detained in London, I understand?' This was true. Matt had been detained – by a surprise farewell party his friends had thrown for him. Fortunately, his mum had been in on the secret and had rearranged his flight.

'Yes, I had some business to sort out before coming here – I told Mr Wu –'

'Oh yes, that is fine. Matt has only missed a couple of days, just settling in, that is all. Welcome to the Beijing International Academy, Matt.'

'Thank you,' said Matt, trying a bow. It must have been the right thing to do, because the receptionist bowed again in return.

'I'll leave you to settle in then,' his mother said. 'Now you remember to work hard, you understand?'

'Yeah, sure,' said Matt. 'Hey, Mum, won't it be great if I get into the martial arts squad?'

'Don't forget that your lessons are the most important thing.'

Matt didn't quite see it this way, but he nodded and said, 'Uh huh.'

'So glad we agree,' said his mother dryly. 'Well, I must go.' She spread out her arms. 'How about a hug for your mum?'

'Er – OK.' Matt hugged her briefly, then stepped back. He would have liked to give her a proper hug, but it was embarrassing with all these kids watching. His mother smiled, as if she knew exactly what he was thinking.

'You've got my number if you want to call. I won't be far away.'

'Sure. Bye, Mum.'

She turned and waved when she reached the

door. The wind-chimes tinkled again, and she was gone.

The receptionist checked a list. 'You will be rooming with Johnny Goldberg.' He looked up and raised his voice. 'Johnny?'

The boy who'd smiled at Matt approached. 'Hi.'

'This is Matt James, your new room-mate. Could you help him settle in?'

'Glad to.' Johnny stuck out his hand and Matt shook it. 'You want to come see the room?'

'Sure,' said Matt.

'Oh, wow!' said Matt for the second time that day.

'Yup. Pretty cool, isn't it?'

The room was large and modern. Two beds stood against opposite walls. There was an en suite bathroom and shower. The floor-to-ceiling window gave on to a superb view of Beijing, a vibrant jumble of ancient and modern buildings as far as Matt could see.

'Some view, huh?' said Johnny. He had an

American accent. 'It's an amazing place, this city. Full of history.'

'You'd get on well with my mum,' said Matt. 'She's crazy about Chinese history.'

'Yeah? So's Shawn Hung – he rooms just opposite, with Olivier. Wanna go and see if they're there? They're great guys – you'll like them.'

'Sure,' said Matt. 'Let's go!'

They crossed the passageway and Johnny tapped on the door facing them. It opened, and there stood a boy, who greeted them with a friendly smile.

'Hi, Shawn. This is my new room-mate Matt – he's just arrived. Thought I'd introduce you guys.'

'Hiya, Matt,' said Shawn. Like Johnny, he had an American accent. 'Come on in!'

A tall, elegant-looking boy was lounging in an armchair. He got up and politely shook Matt's hand. 'Pleased to meet you. I'm Olivier Girard.' He had the lightest trace of a French accent.

The room was every bit as stylish and hi-tech

as Matt's own room, with a similar floor-to-ceiling view of Beijing. A laptop computer sat on a desk, displaying a screen-saver of two martial arts experts going through a sequence of moves: attacking, blocking, counter-attacking.

'Hey,' said Matt. 'I like the screen-saver!'

'Yeah, I put that up myself,' said Shawn. 'You into martial arts?'

'Big time.'

'You any good?'

Matt hesitated. His instructor in London had told him that he was very talented for his age – but the standard at the Academy might be far higher than he was used to. 'I try my best,' he said. 'I've a long way to go before I'd call myself good.'

Shawn nodded. 'I know what you mean. Judo's my sport, by the way.'

That figured. Matt saw that he had just the right physique for judo: he had a low centre of gravity and looked stocky and well balanced.

Matt, being taller with a longer reach, was better equipped for the 'stand-up' forms of combat.

'Mine's tae kwon-do.'

'Cool! We could learn a lot from each other.'

Matt liked Shawn for seeing it like that. 'Yeah,' he agreed. 'I bet we could.'

'Maybe I could join the tutorial then,' said Olivier with a grin. 'I do kung fu.'

'Looks like we've almost got a squad right here!' said Matt. 'How about you, Johnny? Do you do any martial arts?'

Johnny shook his head, grinning. 'Basketball's my game.'

'I thought – don't you have to be tall to be good at basketball?' asked Matt. For a moment he wished he hadn't said it, thinking it might sound rude. But Johnny didn't seem to mind.

'You do need tall guys in the team, for sure,' he said. 'But they don't *all* have to be tall. I can pass and shoot and dribble – I can get right in under the guard of those tall players. I'm hoping to get into the team here.'

'Hope you make it,' said Matt.

Olivier lounged back into his armchair. 'How about you, Matt? Are you gonna try out for the martial arts squad?'

'It's the main reason I wanted to come here,' said Matt.

'Me too!' laughed Olivier.

'Well, good luck,' said Matt. 'I hope you make the squad.'

'Let's hope we all do,' said Shawn. 'Chang Sifu's holding the try-outs tomorrow!'

'What's he like?' asked Matt. He felt nervous and excited at the thought of being taught by the legendary Master Chang. Or Chang Sifu, according to the Chinese way of saying things. Matt knew that studying with Chang was the chance of a lifetime.

'We haven't been coached by him yet – but he's supposed to be hot stuff, from what I've heard,' Shawn replied. 'Mr Wu, the Principal, drafted him in – reckons he's the only guy who can coach us up to the level to beat the Shanghai Academy. You know they've beaten us every time for the last six years? But if anyone can do it, Chang can. He's got quite a reputation.'

Matt nodded. He knew all about Chang Sifu's reputation. The promise of Chang Sifu as coach had made him decide to apply here. He'd looked Chang up on the Internet and found out all about his career. He was a kung fu master, a living martial arts legend – he'd won tournaments all over China. Unlike most kung fu fighters, Chang had studied and mastered other, foreign, forms of fighting. He was a judo black belt, eighth dan, and had even won an Olympic gold medal in the sport. He was a karate black belt too, and an expert in tae kwon-do, aikido, even Thai boxing. He'd won tournaments in all of them. Chang had given up fighting competitively now, but in his whole career, spanning over thirty years, he'd only ever been defeated twice – in any form of martial art.

The sound of an electronically amplified gong, rich and resonant, made Matt jump.

'Hey, that means lunch,' said Johnny. 'The food's pretty good. Let's go meet the others. They're a friendly crowd – mostly. You'll like it here.'

'I like it here already,' said Matt.

'Good morning. My name is Chang Sifu. You may call me Master Chang.'

Matt gazed at him, fascinated. The master was of medium height, and slim. But Matt guessed that Chang would be deadly if he needed to be. His face was virtually unlined, despite his age, and his hair was flecked with grey. He wore a plain white kung fu suit, unadorned except for a black silk belt. He stood with a relaxed air, arms hanging by his sides – yet there was a suggestion of hidden readiness, as though at any moment he might explode into action.

Matt and the others stood in a respectful

semi-circle at the edge of the mat. The *kwoon*
– or training hall – was the centre of the
Academy's amazing gymnasium. Matt had felt
excited when he read about it in the prospectus,
but being here was something else. There
was a weights room, a gym with vaults, bars
and beams, a swimming pool, squash courts,
basketball courts and even a five-a-side football
pitch. The Beijing International Academy
offered a full range of sports beside martial arts.
But it was the *kwoon* that was the beating heart
of the place. Today was the day of the try-outs.
Matt's own heart was beating fast.

Chang didn't begin with the tryouts. First, he
made the group do some stretching exercises.
Then he said, 'Before the try-outs, let us practise a
basic block technique.' He spoke softly but clearly.
His English was fluent but slightly accented. 'To
defend against strike, like so –' he thrust out a
hand with blinding speed – 'we employ two-
handed block, like so.' He changed stance and

brought up his arms, wrists together. Matt knew similar moves from tae kwon-do, but he had never seen them executed with such speed and grace. 'Equally effective against kicks, strikes and punches,' said Chang. 'In pairs, please, find a space on mat. Take in turns to strike then block.'

Matt found himself paired with Catarina Ribeiro. He had met her at lunch with Johnny yesterday and they'd got on well. She was a Brazilian girl, taller than Matt, with long black hair – tied back today – and dark brown eyes. She moved with the fluid grace of a dancer, and had originally trained in the dance form of the South American martial art capoeira, before taking lessons in the combat form of the art – without telling her father.

'But wouldn't your dad be mad if he found out?' Johnny had asked.

'Yes,' replied Catarina with a laugh. 'But he won't find out!' Matt and Johnny had joined in the laughter; Catarina's giggle was infectious.

Master Chang clapped his hands. 'Bow to your partner – and begin.'

'Do you want to go first?' asked Matt.

'Sure, why not?' said Catarina – and immediately struck out at Matt. She was fast; he only just got the block up in time.

'Hey, you're good!' he told her.

Catarina smiled. 'You too. You block fast.'

He and Catarina soon fell into a steady rhythm: attack, block; block, attack. Out of the corner of his eye Matt noticed Chang going around quietly watching each pair in turn, sometimes correcting a stance with a touch on the shoulder, sometimes demonstrating the strike or block again, but never saying a word. When he came to Matt and Catarina he watched for a while, then nodded and moved away. Matt felt a glow of pride, and so, to judge by her expression, did Catarina.

Master Chang returned to the centre of the *tatami* – a large square white mat, firm but springy. He clapped his hands. 'Now it is time for try-outs. Let me first explain. The eleven most promising fighters will be selected for this year's squad.'

Matt did a quick scan-count of all the kids in the room. There were just over fifty. He let out a slow breath, as he realized he only had around a one-in-five chance of making it.

'The squad is to compete in the Divisional Championship,' Chang went on. 'This Championship is mixed combat – that is, a variety of styles is permitted. Facing an opponent of unfamiliar style may cause problems. A fighter from tradition such as ju–jitsu or judo against stand-up kung fu or karate fighter finds he has to defend against strikes and kicks and cannot get to close quarters to perform a throw. Or a karate fighter drawn into close quarters cannot use repertoire of strikes; once on the floor he is helpless. For this reason the complete martial artist should have working knowledge of both take-down and stand-up styles. For try-outs you will each fight two bouts: one against fighter of same or similar style to your own; one against fighter of contrasting tradition.

'Before we begin, let us ready ourselves. Stand still, relax, drop shoulders. Breathe slowly in, out, in, out. You are sleeping tigers. Soon tiger will awake. Now, it rests.'

Matt let his shoulders drop. He felt his sinews relax as he breathed deeply in and out. He was a powerful tiger, the great muscles at rest beneath the striped fur . . .

'What is this garbage?' he heard a voice beside him mutter. 'Sleeping tigers – that's kids' stuff. Let's get on with the fighting!'

The voice belonged to Carl Warrick, a big blonde Australian boy. Matt had heard him the day before, bragging about his prowess at karate. He'd spoken under his breath just now, but Master Chang's eyes flicked towards him instantly. Chang said nothing, but slowly raised a finger to his lips. Carl looked down at the mat.

Calm descended once again. Master Chang waited. Then he clapped his hands.

'First bout,' he said softly. 'Carl Warrick against Stephane Krupps.'

The two boys faced each other on the mat and bowed. The fight began.

Stephane, like Carl, was a karateka. But it was clear from the word go that he was outclassed. Carl's boasts about his skill had not been empty. He swept aside Stephane's defence, bearing him backwards and raining down blows; then he swept his legs from under him and Stephane was down on the mat, gasping for breath.

Master Chang raised his hand to signal that the bout was over. But to Matt's surprise, Carl took no notice. He grabbed Stephane by his tunic and hauled him to his feet.

'That was too easy, kid. Let's go again!'

'No,' said Chang, without raising his voice. He strode forward. 'Your father is famous karate

17

champion,' he said. 'Member of Australian Olympic team.'

'That's right,' said Carl.

'I have seen him compete. He has good technique and great spirit.' There was a pause. 'Your father would be ashamed of you today,' said Chang.

Carl flushed.

'In martial arts you must respect your opponent. Today you were stronger, but one day you will meet an opponent stronger than yourself. Bow to Stephane, Carl.'

Carl bowed jerkily and went back to his place. 'Next bout,' said Chang serenely. 'Lars Pedder and Shawn Hung.'

Matt watched, hoping to see his friend do well. Shawn and Lars tussled, gripping each other's jackets. Lars was bigger than Shawn and seemed to have the advantage – but suddenly Shawn bent his knees, wedged his hip against Lars and with one quick movement sent him

crashing to the mat. Matt gave Shawn a quick
thumbs-up as he returned to his place, grinning.

Soon it was Matt's turn. He was matched
against a boy called Bruno, another tae kwon-do
practitioner. Bruno was big and looked strong.
He started aggressively with a series of forward
punches. Matt blocked them all. He began
to feel confident – Bruno was strong, but he
made it so obvious what he was going to do
next, Matt had no problem in countering.
Bruno twisted his body away from Matt and
delivered a back kick. Clearly this was supposed
to take Matt by surprise, but he blocked it
easily. Then, as Bruno turned back towards
him, Matt delivered a high crescent kick which
broke Bruno's guard, then followed it with two
forward punches to Bruno's chest. Bruno backed
off and Matt followed in with a beautiful, high
axe kick, again smashing through Bruno's guard.
Bruno gave ground, then tried to retaliate
with a reverse turning kick. Matt blocked this

19

one-handed, and hit Bruno in the ribs with a well-timed side-kick. Bruno staggered and sat down hard on the mat.

Chang clapped. 'Enough. Well fought.' He signalled a win for Matt by gesturing towards him with an open hand.

Matt and Bruno bowed to each other and returned to their places.

'You fight good!' Catarina said to him. Matt felt pleased. He knew he'd fought well, but he also felt the harder test was still to come. Against a tae kwon-do opponent he was in his element. Fighting against unfamiliar techniques would be a different ball-game.

More bouts followed in quick succession. Matt was glad to see that Shawn won his second bout, and Olivier won both of his. Catarina won too. Before Matt knew it, his turn had come around again.

This time he was matched against a red-haired German boy, Wolfgang. Wolfgang was shorter than Matt, but very strongly built. With his barrel chest and small round head he looked like a miniature bull. He was a ju-jitsu specialist. Matt had watched him win his previous fight and knew he was an opponent to be reckoned with.

Matt had barely taken his stance after bowing before Wolfgang dropped his head low and charged at him. Matt got in a glancing punch on Wolfgang's shoulder – but now Wolfgang was in close. He grabbed Matt's jacket and pushed him backwards, trying to hook his leg round Matt's. Matt fought as best he could, but it was all he could do to keep his balance. He wasn't used to this kind of combat.

Suddenly he noticed that his hip was in contact with Wolfgang's stomach. The throw Shawn had used earlier flashed into his mind. He bent his knees, twisted his hip and straightened up. Wolfgang was pulled off his feet and rolled over Matt's back. He crashed to the floor.

Master Chang signalled the win.

'You did well,' he said quietly to Matt. 'You show flexibility. Adaptability. That is good.'

Glowing from the fight and Chang's praise, Matt went and stood next to Shawn. 'That was thanks to you,' he said.

'I said we could learn from each other, didn't I?'

'You did,' said Matt. 'Thanks! Maybe I'll teach you some kicks!'

That evening, the list of squad members was posted up on the notice-board outside the refectory. A huge crowd of students gathered around it. Matt, Catarina, Olivier and Shawn elbowed their way to the front.

'Yes!' said Matt. There was his name – **MATT JAMES** – in bold black type.

Catarina's name was there too. So was Olivier's. And so was Shawn's.

They all exchanged high fives.

'Hey, what's this – the list's up?' said a loud Australian voice. 'My name better be on it!'

It was Carl Warrick. He jostled his way to the front. 'Glad to see Chang's got some sense,' he said, peering at the notice-board. 'But why am I at the bottom of the list? I should be at the top!'

'It's alphabetical,' said Matt. Everyone laughed.

Carl clenched his jaw. 'I knew that!' he said. 'I was just kidding.'

Shawn turned to Matt. 'How about we go to the *kwoon* now and put in a bit of practice? You could teach me those kicks you were talking about.'

'Sure thing,' said Matt.

'Let's all go!' said Olivier.

'How about you, Carl?' said Matt. Carl wasn't his favourite person, but they were all on the same team together. 'Want to come? We could teach each other a few moves.'

'No, thanks,' said Carl. 'There's nothing you lot can teach me.'

'Except manners, maybe?' said Catarina, smiling sweetly.

Chapter

2

THE JADE DISH

'Hey, Mum! Guess what — I made the team!' said
Matt into his mobile.

'That's great news, Matt. I hope you're
working hard at your lessons too.'

'Oh . . . yeah. Of course.' Matt was halfway
through the second week now. So far, the classes
hadn't been too bad. The teachers made the
lessons fun, and were not over-strict, but it was
the martial arts training that Matt really looked
forward to every day. 'Anyway, about the squad,
Mum — we're training for the match against the
Shanghai Academy. I know we can beat them.

We've got a great squad – there's Shawn, and
Catarina, and Olivier . . .'

Matt took a deep breath as he thought about
how determined he and his new friends were
to win the Championship for the Academy.
They talked about it all the time. They trained
together. They taught each other moves. Matt
had never had such fun. Because his mother was
an ambassador, Matt had moved around a lot,
changing schools every couple of years. Now,
for the first time he felt like he really belonged;
he was part of a group of friends all working
together for the same goal. It was funny, but five
thousand miles away from London he felt more
at home than he ever had before.

'I'm glad to hear you've made so many
friends,' said his mother. 'Listen, I have to
go now. I've got a lunch appointment at the
embassy. Love you.'

'Love you too,' said Matt, and clicked his
mobile shut. He sometimes wished he and his

mum had more time together, to talk face to face. Then again, he knew it was his mum's job that gave him the chance to train under the brilliant Chang.

Matt turned round to find Carl Warrick standing there with two of his cronies, Miles and Roger. They were all grinning.

'Who do you love, James?' said Carl. 'Was that your girlfriend?'

'My mother,' said Matt coldly.

'Ah, diddums – he loves his mummy!'

Miles and Roger sniggered.

Matt considered telling Carl he wasn't worth answering, then decided it wasn't even worth saying that. He spied Johnny, Shawn and Olivier on the other side of the common room and went over to join them.

'Hey, Matt. Were those idiots giving you a hard time?' asked Johnny.

Matt shrugged. 'I just ignore them.'

Catarina came in through the door at the far

end of the common room. She had an unusual way of walking, a loose-jointed, long-legged stride, and as she came over to Matt's group, Carl whispered something to his cronies and began to follow her. He mimicked her stride, stretching out his legs exaggeratedly. Miles and Roger laughed.

'Those idiots,' said Olivier. 'Do you think we should –'

'No need,' said Matt. 'She can look after herself.'

Catarina, hearing the laughter, stopped and turned to face Carl.

'Something wrong?'

'Hey, lanky,' said Carl. Catarina was hardly taller than he was, but her slim frame and long legs made her height more noticeable. 'I was just wondering what the view's like up there.'

Catarina smiled. 'The view is fine,' she said. 'At least it was until you came along to spoil it.'

She spoke so gently that it took Carl a second to realize he'd been insulted. Then he scowled, stuck his hands in his pockets and slouched off, his cronies following.

Matt and his friends laughed. 'Good one, Catarina!' said Matt.

Johnny glanced at his watch. 'Break's nearly over, you guys. Come on – we don't want to be late for history.'

'Oh – don't we?' said Matt, and they all laughed again, scuffling and breaking into mock combat as they made their way to class.

Mr Figgis, the history teacher, was English but had a deep love of all things Chinese.

'The Chinese have a marvellously rich culture – rich in art, architecture, literature, music, dance … Their civilization was at a highly advanced level when Europe was still in the Dark Ages. When Marco Polo, the European explorer, came here in the twelfth century he was amazed at what he saw. The Chinese invented paper, and gunpowder – and fireworks, of course.

'In these classes we are going to learn the history of the great dynasties of the Chinese emperors – and the wars, upheavals and revolutions that have visited this vast and complex country over the centuries.'

Matt listened with interest. It was impossible not to be infected with Mr Figgis's enthusiasm. Johnny was clearly fascinated, his eyes shining behind his glasses. And Chinese-American Shawn Hung glowed with pride at hearing the country of his ancestors praised. Only Carl, Matt noticed, looked bored. He lounged in his seat, lip curled, looking out of the window.

'But before we get on to the gory bits,' Mr Figgis continued, 'I want you all to have a taste of the marvellous things this culture has to offer. That's why I've organized a field trip for next week. We're going to the Palace Museum, in the Forbidden City. It's in the heart of Beijing, where the great emperors used to rule. You'll see wonderful things there: sculptures, statues, paintings, armour, weapons. But, most interesting from your point of view, you'll see the Emperor's Jade Dish. This is a priceless artefact – and, as you may know, a replica of it is awarded to the winner of the Divisional Championship. The Shanghai Academy has held it for the last six years – but we're going to get it back this year, aren't we, Carl?' said Figgis, abruptly turning his attention on Carl, who was still staring out of the window.

'What? I'll win my fight, that's for sure,' Carl said. 'I can't answer for the other guys.'

'Yeah, I'll win my fight, no problem, 'cause I'm the great Carl Warrick!' said Olivier, in a perfect imitation of Carl's sullen drawl. The whole class erupted into laughter. Carl shot a look of pure venom at Olivier, who grinned.

'That's enough,' said Mr Figgis. 'Now, Catarina, if you wouldn't mind handing out these textbooks for me . . .'

★

'Hey, I've had an idea!' said Matt that evening. 'The Palace Museum – they must have a website, right?'

'I guess,' said Johnny.

It was after supper, an hour before lights-out, and they were in their room relaxing after a strenuous day. Johnny had made it through the basketball try-outs and on to the team, so he was feeling pretty pleased with himself. Matt was glad for his friend – he knew how much it meant to him. His thoughts drifted to the trip to the museum. He couldn't wait to see the original of the Jade Dish, a replica of which, with any luck – no, with determination and serious training – the squad would bring back to the Beijing International Academy. And now it occurred to him, maybe he didn't have to wait.

'Let's have a look. Maybe it'll show some of the, you know, artefacts. The Jade Dish.'

'Cool!' said Johnny, sitting down at the computer. A few moments later he had the

Palace Museum website up on the screen. *Click here for Interactive Virtual Tour*, it said.

'Go on then,' said Matt. 'Click.'

Johnny clicked. The screen displayed a gallery, lined on either side by life-sized jade warriors.

'Look at those!' said Johnny. 'Aren't they cool?'

'Yeah, but keep going,' Matt said.

A few more rooms, and they came to it. It stood on a plinth, enclosed in a glass case. It sat beneath a spotlight and shone a deep, vivid green.

'Can you zoom in on it?'

'Sure.'

Johnny double-clicked and the Jade Dish filled the screen. Two imperial dragons were intertwined in the centre, their fierce, round-eyed faces staring out at the viewer. The dish was edged with ornate gold patterns and underneath the dragons was an inscription in Chinese characters. Matt couldn't read Chinese but the elegant strokes etched themselves into his mind. He let out a long breath.

'Just think – the Academy team could be holding that up after the Championship!'

'Holding up the replica,' Johnny corrected him.

'OK, the replica – what's the difference!'

Matt walked over to the window and looked out at the city. It was ablaze with light. Somewhere in the heart of that city of millions of people, was the Forbidden City, and within the Forbidden City was the Palace Museum, and within the Palace Museum was the Emperor's Jade Dish. Matt's fingers tingled as he imagined standing with his team-mates, holding up the replica dish after the tournament. 'Please,' he whispered to himself, 'please let us win.'

The next morning, Mr Wu made a surprising announcement in Assembly. Mr Wu was small, middle-aged and always impeccably dressed in a dark, well-cut suit and tie. He wore tiny steel spectacles and a pencil-thin moustache. His English was careful and precise.

'Master Chang tells me that he has selected the squad for the Divisional Championship. I should like to take this opportunity to wish you all the very best of luck. This school has a proud record in martial arts competitions, but in recent years, despite fine individual performances, we have failed to regain the trophy from the Shanghai Academy. This year, under Master Chang's tutelage, I count on you to put that right.

'Which brings me to an announcement from Master Chang. For today's training session, would the squad report to the swimming pool at thirteen hundred hours, wearing combat attire. I repeat, the swimming pool, not the *kwoon*. Thank you.'

Matt wrinkled his brow. 'The swimming pool?' he said to Shawn. 'In our martial arts suits?'

'Weird,' said Shawn.

Carl let everyone know what he thought as soon as Assembly was over.

'What's the guy playing at? It's crazy! Are we training for a water polo tournament, or what?'

'He must have his reasons,' said Shawn.

'Yeah, crazy reasons,' said Carl. 'The guy's a couple of prawns short of a barbie, if you ask me!'

'But nobody is asking you,' said Catarina.

Eleven surfboards stood against the tiled wall of the swimming pool.

'All students please take one,' said Chang.

'Er – why?' said Carl.

'That should not be difficult to work out. Here are surfboards; there is pool. I wish you to stand on surfboards in pool.'

'In our martial arts suits? Why not swimming trunks, if we're playing water games?'

'There is a simple answer to your question,' said Chang mildly. 'If you are clothed, you have incentive to remain dry.'

Matt took his board, lowered it on to the water and carefully stepped on to it. It dipped at once, and Matt swiftly adjusted his stance to steady it. He floated out into the middle of the pool. Other students followed suit – they were wobbling, bending and flailing, but all managed to remain upright. Matt noticed that Catarina was easily the best at it. She stood as straight and still as if she was on dry land.

The motion of the other boards created wavelets that made Matt's board rock. He kept having to make adjustments, shifting his weight. He couldn't afford not to concentrate; all his muscles were in a state of readiness, anticipating the next movement.

'What's the *point* of this?' Carl's voice echoed loudly around the room.

'To perfect balance.'

'Yeah, well, my balance is perfect already, so –'

But Carl had forgotten to concentrate. His board began to tip. He hastily over-corrected, wobbled and slipped into the pool with a cry.

Olivier burst out laughing, and the next moment he had also lost his balance. He plunged into the water. Matt looked down at him and had to force himself not to laugh as he watched his friend frantically dog-paddling, his dark hair plastered over his forehead. Olivier saw the smile that flitted over Matt's face and grabbed the edge of Matt's board. Matt fell headlong into the water.

He rose to the surface, spluttering, and splashed water at Olivier in retaliation. Olivier grinned and splashed back. Then they swam to Shawn's board and tipped him off. Carl, meanwhile, got his own back on Catarina by swimming underneath her board and pushing upwards, so that she toppled off, squealing. All around, kids were falling or pulling each other into the pool. A wild water-fight broke out, with splashing, ducking and shouts of laughter.

Matt surfaced and caught sight of Master Chang standing at the poolside, watching them. Matt couldn't tell if the glint in Chang's eye meant he was angry or amused. Matt trod water, waiting for the next instruction.

'Back on to your boards,' said Chang

37

eventually, giving nothing away. Matt scrambled back up on to the wet, slippery surface. It was time to start learning again.

The following day in the *kwoon*, Matt found out just how hard Master Chang was prepared to make them work.

'Find space on mat, please. You need two clear steps in front of you, two clear steps behind. Today we do training exercise, designed to improve speed and stamina. It is adapted from a basic kata. Kata is a sequence of movements in karate, to be performed without partner –'

'I know what a kata is, thanks!' said Carl. 'I've been doing them since I was four.'

'Then perhaps you will find this exercise easy,' said Chang. 'Let us see. Please watch and listen, everybody.' He proceeded to perform each movement as he talked his way through the sequence. 'Step forward to left. Lunge punch with left hand, like so. Aim to make contact with

imaginary opponent. Now step back to original
position. Step forward to right. Lunge punch
with right hand. Step back to original position.
Step back with left foot. Kick with right, like so.
Step forward to original position. Step back with
right foot. Kick with left. Step back to original
position. Sequence is ended and ready to repeat.
This is all clear?'

Matt and his friends nodded.

'Then perform sequence ten times.' Chang
clapped his hands.

Matt began the sequence, slowly at first,
building speed as he got used to the movements.
Chang went around, correcting students where
necessary. Carl was the first to finish. Chang was
busy with another student as Carl completed
the last step, but their master called out without
even turning round, 'Ten more, Carl!'

Matt reached the end of his ten and again,
without even looking, Chang called out, 'Ten
more, Matt!'

It was uncanny. Master Chang seemed to have such a good sense of how fast everyone was working that without needing to look he knew when each student was on the tenth repetition. 'Ten more, Catarina!' 'Ten more, Shawn!' 'Ten more, Lola!' 'Ten more, Olivier!' 'Ten more, Wolfgang!'

By the end of his second ten, Matt was breathing hard, but enjoying himself. The sequence felt instinctive and he was putting everything into it. By the end of the fourth ten he was beginning to tire. His muscles were aching and he was slowing down. By the end of the sixth he was seriously tired. His muscles were trembling and his breathing laboured. He had to work harder to concentrate on the steps of the sequence. By the end of the eighth he was ready to drop.

'Ten more, Matt!'

Matt groaned inwardly, but began the sequence again. He wasn't the only one who was exhausted. Looking around he saw Olivier panting for breath, Shawn grimacing in pain. Catarina's long hair flopped over her face and she was too tired to push it away. Carl, who had started faster than any of them, was performing the moves in slow motion now.

'Ten more, Carl!'

Carl stopped abruptly. He stood with his arms dangling at his sides, red-faced and sweaty, panting for breath. 'Look, I must have done this a hundred times –'

'This is the last ten.'

Sullenly, Carl started again. But at the end of the last repetition, Chang sang out, 'Ten more, Carl!'

'What?' said Carl angrily. 'But you said –'

'It is the unexpected effort that is hardest to make,' said Chang.

'This is a joke!' shouted Carl. 'I can't do any more!'

He stormed out of the *kwoon*. As he ran past, Matt saw there were tears in his eyes.

'I will speak to Carl later,' said Chang. 'He will learn in his own time. And now,' he clapped his hands. 'Ten more, everybody!'

When the session finally came to an end, Matt flopped to the floor. So did the others. Matt saw Olivier lying about a metre away.

'Are we still alive?' he croaked.

'I think so,' said Olivier. 'But only just.'

'I pushed you hard today,' said Master Chang. 'But there is a reason. I need to see how much you want to win; I need to see if spirit is stronger than body. In combat you may be tired like today, ready to give in. If you give in, fight is lost. But maybe opponent is as tired as you; if you continue, you can win. Technique alone will not serve against opponent who also has good technique. You need spirit. I can teach you technique. I cannot teach you spirit. But today? I teach you *need* for spirit.'

MEMORY GAMES

'I have an announcement to make,' said Mr Wu in Assembly the next morning. 'Your trip to the Palace Museum is postponed until further notice.'

A mutter of disappointment rippled through the hall.

'The Palace Museum informs me there has been a break-in,' said Mr Wu. 'Thieves disabled the security system, entered the museum at night and stole some items. Nothing of extraordinary value, thank goodness. The thieves do not seem to have had a clear idea of what they were looking for. They stole only a collection of old copper coins, practically worthless, and –' Mr Wu's mouth appeared to twitch for a moment as if suppressing a smile – 'some postcards from the museum shop. The museum will be closed to the public while an investigation is carried out.'

Matt noticed that Shawn, who was standing next to him, looked stunned. Was he upset that the trip had been postponed? It was disappointing, of course – but Shawn looked really put out.

'You OK, Shawn?'

'I – yeah, I'm fine,' he mumbled unconvincingly.

Matt didn't have a chance to question Shawn further until the morning's lessons were over. At break, Matt and his friends went to the canteen for a snack.

'What's up, Shawn?' asked Matt. 'You look like you've had a shock.'

44

Shawn looked down at the table. 'Know who designed that security system in the museum?'

'No – who?'

'My father, that's who.'

'Oh,' said Matt. 'Right.'

'Maybe – there was some sort of glitch,' said Johnny. 'It happens.'

'Happens all the time,' said Olivier.

Shawn shook his head. 'Not with my dad's systems. He knows what he's doing. That system was the best in the world – my dad told me!'

'Then how did the thieves get in?' said Catarina.

'There's only one explanation. They must have planned this carefully; they must have been computer experts – they'd have to be geniuses to get past that system –'

'Yeah, that must be it,' said Matt, trying his best to cheer Shawn up.

A raucous laugh broke out nearby. It was Carl, with Miles and Roger tagging along.

45

'Did I hear that right? Your dad built the burglar alarm?'

'It isn't a burglar alarm, it is a state-of-the-art security system –'

'So state-of-the-art that a bunch of clueless bozos walked straight through it?'

'They weren't clueless!'

'That's what it says here,' said Carl, and held up a copy of the English-language newspaper, *The Beijing Times*. CLUELESS THIEVES STEAL COINS AND CARDS, the headline announced.

'I reckon the Palace Museum might be asking your dad for their money back!' said Carl, and walked off laughing with Miles and Roger in tow.

'Ignore them,' said Matt. 'They're just idiots.' He laid his hand on Shawn's shoulder.

Shawn shook his head. 'Forget it,' he said. 'Just forget it!'

★

The thing about Master Chang's training
sessions was that you never knew what to
expect. Matt arrived at the next day's session
prepared for another gruelling workout. But
Chang surprised him, and everyone else, by
calmly announcing that they were going for a
walk.

'A walk!' said Carl. 'Er – *why*?'

Master Chang didn't answer this. 'Change
out of martial arts suits, please. You will not
need them. For this expedition, civilian dress is
required.'

The walk led them out of the Academy and to
a bustling local market in Jade Moon Street.

'Follow me,' said Chang. 'And keep your eyes
open.'

Matt had always thought London was a busy
city. But, compared to Beijing, London was
only half full. Here, there were crowds of people
queuing at the market stalls, queuing to get
into bars and restaurants, and even queuing up

to cross the road. Through the crowds, hordes of cyclists made their way, ringing their bells and shouting at people who didn't move aside quickly enough.

There were stalls selling fruit, stalls selling flowers, stalls selling noodles and mobile phones and MP3 players. Matt had always had a keen eye for detail and as he walked through the milling crowds he clocked image after image, storing them away in his memory. An old man with an eye-patch. A party of American tourists taking photos, led by a man in loud check trousers. A group of tall Chinese teenagers in tracksuits. A wizened old lady at a stall selling trainers. A little boy eating a peach with the juice dribbling down his chin . . .

At last, Master Chang led them into a quiet side street. Here they rested beneath the shade of a tree.

'Let us see how wide open you kept your eyes.

Near start of market, there was a stall with young flower-girl. What colour sash did she wear?'

'Orange,' said Matt.

Chang nodded. The others looked at Matt in surprise.

'Olivier – man walking dog nearly bumped into you. Was he holding leash in left hand or right hand?'

'Left, I think – no, right?'

Chang looked at Matt.

'It was the left hand,' said Matt. 'The man was wearing a T-shirt with a picture of Bill Gates on it. The dog was a big white fluffy one.'

'A chow, that is correct. Did anyone see youth basketball team?'

'I did,' volunteered Olivier. 'Bunch of tall guys in tracksuits.'

'There were seven of them,' added Matt. 'The tracksuits were blue with a white stripe down the sleeve.'

'You have sharp eyes, Matt,' said Chang.

'Oh, well, I . . . I just notice things, that's all,' said Matt, embarrassed to be praised in front of the others.

'I noticed things too!' protested Carl. 'You're just not asking me about them.'

'Then what did you notice, Carl?'

'Er – a lot of people on bikes.'

There were a few grins at this. Chang did not smile, but gravely said, 'Yes, there were bikes. Now, one of the last stalls we passed was fruit stall with line of apples on display along front. How many apples?'

Matt knew the answer to this one too. Twelve. But he saw that Shawn was about to speak, and kept quiet. Shawn had had to put up with a lot of jokes since the news about his father had got out, and getting a question right might cheer him up.

'There were twelve,' said Shawn.

'A good answer,' said Chang. He turned to Catarina. 'Is he right?'

To Matt's surprise, Catarina appeared flustered. It was the first time he'd seen her at a loss for words. 'He . . . he's sort of right,' she said, after an awkward pause. 'And he's sort of not.'

'Why is that?'

'Because – because the twelfth one is here,' said Catarina, and produced an apple from her pocket.

How on earth had Chang managed to spot that? Matt wondered. Matt hadn't seen Catarina take the apple himself – and Chang had been in front of them.

'I am not really a thief,' said Catarina. 'I mean, not a proper one. It is just . . . I do this sometimes. For a laugh, you know? For a joke . . .'

Her voice trailed away. Chang raised his eyebrows.

'OK, OK, I will take it back!'

Catarina ran back to the stall to return the apple.

'The walk is ended,' said Chang. 'Let us go.'

51

They walked back through the market, picking up Catarina again on the way. Shawn fell into step with Matt. 'Hey, man, I'm impressed. You've got a photographic memory!'

'Like I said, I just tend to notice things.'

'The whole thing's stupid!' said Carl loudly. 'This isn't martial arts training, it's just a waste of time!'

He said this loud enough for Chang to hear, but Chang did not respond. Carl refused to give up. 'Come on, sir, tell us – what's the point of all these games? How's it gonna help us win the tournament?'

'You will learn in time,' Chang said.

'If you tell me now I'll learn right away!'

'If I tell you now, it will mean little to you. True understanding comes only when you learn for yourself.'

Carl lapsed into a sulky silence. Matt thought about Master Chang's words. Though he couldn't work out Chang's methods any more than Carl could, he felt sure that in time he would understand. There was something mesmerizing about Chang, something in his quiet calm and assurance that convinced Matt he had good reasons for everything he did. It was hard to see how, but somehow Matt trusted that Chang's methods would help them beat the Shanghai Academy.

There were only six weeks to go before the tournament.

Matt couldn't wait.

Chapter 4

FIELD TRIP

'Hold your partner firmly in armlock,' said Master Chang. 'Now, partner, you have one hand free. Strike to body, once, twice – not full force, we do not want broken ribs – and pull away!'

Matt, who was being armlocked by Olivier, dealt him two blows to the side and pulled his other arm away swiftly. Olivier's hold slackened and Matt was free. Today Chang was teaching them some ju-jitsu holds often used by the Shanghai team, and how to counter them.

It was four weeks into the term now and Matt had developed a great respect for Chang's

training methods. He looked forward to the
sessions more than anything. You never knew
what to expect. Sometimes there were strange,
interesting activities that it was hard to see the
point of at first, but which always made you
think. Sometimes there was fitness work. Then
sometimes, like today, Chang would drill them
on the real nitty-gritty of fighting techniques
– and even Carl had to admit that here Chang
Sifu knew his stuff. Today's session had left them
all gasping for breath.

Chang clapped his hands. 'Remember,' he said,
'if you find yourself in such a hold, strike fast
and hard and try to pull free at the same time
– opponent reacting to blow is not concentrating
on hold. Wait only one second and the hold
tightens again.' He paused. 'You have worked
hard today. Relax. Sit.'

Matt and the others sat down on the *tatami*.
Matt sat near Olivier, Shawn and Catarina. The
four of them had become close friends and

always hung out together. Johnny sometimes hung out with them too, but he spent a lot of time working hard in the library and when he wasn't doing that he was usually to be found shooting hoops with his basketball team-mates. It was a pity that Johnny wasn't free to join them more often, but Matt was tolerant of his friend's eccentric preference for basketball; after all, not everyone could be a martial arts fanatic.

It was a relief to rest after such a hard workout. The *kwoon* was cool, air-conditioned. The walls were white with high, tinted windows through which Matt could see the skyscrapers of Beijing. Chang sat facing his squad, legs crossed, back straight.

'So,' said Chang. 'Let us talk.'

'What about?' said Carl.

'What you wish. You may ask me questions.'

'Tell us about the Shanghai Academy team, sir,' said Shawn. 'What are they like?'

'They are well trained. They are highly

competitive. They have been known to use rough tactics.'

'How do you mean, rough tactics?' asked Matt, concerned. He wasn't scared, but he hated unfairness.

'Illegal blows. Do not worry. With defences you have practised you can protect yourselves. Above all, do not be tempted to reply in kind. You must fight honourably, within rules.'

'But how come they don't get disqualified?' asked Matt.

'They are cunning, striking when the judges' view is blocked. But they do not rely entirely on illegal blows. They are a highly trained, formidable team, capable of winning fairly too.'

'But we can beat them, right?' That was Shawn.

'It is possible. You have one advantage.'

'What's that?' asked Matt.

'Shanghai team trainer, Sensei Johnson, rules by *fear*. His team are highly motivated – but very afraid to lose. It is not good to be motivated by fear.'

'What's he like, this Sensei Johnson?' asked Carl. 'What's his martial art speciality?'

'He is a karateka. An American, now retired from competitive fights. In his day, he might have been considered expert in certain techniques.'

'He's not as good as you though, is he, sir?' said Shawn.

Chang smiled. 'I am an old man, now.'

'Tell us about some of your fights,' said Matt. 'You were the best, weren't you?'

'Not at all,' said Chang unexpectedly. 'The best fighter I ever witnessed was my grandfather.'

'Your grandfather?' prompted Catarina.

'Oh yes. I learned much from him. Though not all he had to teach. He was a famous kung fu fighter, known throughout China. He was leader of elite fighting team – the Tangshan Tigers!'

The name caused a twinge of excitement in Matt. The Tangshan Tigers. He had a vision of a team of crack fighters – dedicated, proud, invincible.

'Great,' muttered Carl. 'Family history – that's all we need.'

Chang suddenly directed a look like a laser beam at Carl. 'You are speaking of my ancestor, Carl. You will please to show respect.'

Carl flushed, and looked down at the mat. 'Sorry,' he mumbled.

Matt knew by now that Chang would never rule his team by fear. But he could certainly be scary when he wanted to make his point.

The next morning, Mr Figgis came into the history class with a broad smile on his face.

'I have some excellent news for you, boys and girls. The Forbidden City Palace Museum has now reopened. We'll be making our trip tomorrow and we'll spend the whole day there.'

'Yes!' said Matt. There was clapping and whooping all around the class. A day off school,

missing maths, English and double science, was
something to celebrate.

'Cool!' said Johnny, his eyes shining. Matt
guessed that he wasn't just pleased because of
the day off; he was looking forward to seeing the
treasures of China's past. Matt felt some of the
same anticipation. He couldn't wait to see the
Emperor's Jade Dish up close – with any luck, he
thought, he'd soon be holding his very own jade
dish. The tournament trophy!

It was a bright, crisp autumn morning as Matt's
class piled excitedly on to the school coach – a
luxury gleaming silver double-decker with
air-conditioning and tables between the seats.
Matt and his friends made straight for the upper
deck. They had a great view of the city from
here, with its busy streets and towering hi-tech
skyscrapers.

The journey passed quickly, as they pointed
at things through the window, chatting and

laughing and joking. Catarina shared out some sweets that she had smuggled aboard.

Soon the coach was stopping at the top of a huge public square.

'This is Tiananmen Square, everybody!' called Mr Figgis. 'This is where we get off!'

Matt and his mates ran downstairs.

'Slow down!' said Mr Figgis. He was a short, slightly tubby man with wispy fair hair and a tweed jacket. 'Two straight lines, please! Two straight lines!'

He led them through an arched gate, and along a busy thoroughfare lined on both sides with souvenir stalls. Another imposing gate greeted them at the end, where a uniformed guard checked the ticket Mr Figgis showed. He nodded and they passed through into the Forbidden City.

Matt looked around. They were in a spacious courtyard, with huge marble palaces, decorated with carvings of dragons, of cranes, of clouds, of torches and of tortoises. After the skyscrapers of modern Beijing, it was like stepping back in time.

'That's the Palace Museum!' said Mr Figgis, pointing to one of the larger and more ornate buildings at the far end.

They walked up the broad marble steps. A museum official was waiting to greet them in the entrance hall. He was a thin, rather weedy-looking man with a straggling moustache and protruding front teeth. He wore a dark suit with a name-badge on the lapel which said MR PEI: ASSISTANT CURATOR.

He bowed politely. 'You are the Beijing International Academy?'

'Yes, indeed!' said Mr Figgis, bowing in return.

'Welcome. We are most sorry for postponing your visit. You will be pleased to know that everything is back to normal. The security system is functioning once more, and our Board of Directors will be reviewing the situation to see if it needs an upgrade. But rest assured you may enjoy your tour in perfect safety.'

Matt saw Shawn's jaw tighten at the mention

of his father's security system. Shawn didn't speak, but Miles did. Miles was one of Carl's cronies. He didn't do any martial arts, but if sneering had been a competitive sport, he would have been a black belt.

'Hey, I'll tell you something funny!' he said loudly. 'This guy here' – he patted Shawn on the shoulder – 'his dad designed your security system! The one that doesn't work properly and needs an upgrade!'

Shawn looked as though he was about to explode. Matt gave him a sympathetic glance. Mr Pei coughed in embarrassment, covering his mouth with his hand.

'Er, as I say, the system is under review. Shall we commence our tour?'

The class followed Mr Pei into the museum. Matt looked again at Shawn. His eyes were glued to the floor and Matt hoped that Shawn didn't feel too bad. He hadn't known Shawn for long, but he hated to see his friend so unhappy.

THE TIGERS ARE FORMED

The rooms of the museum were wide, with high ceilings. Everyone's footsteps echoed. Matt felt as though he was walking through a cathedral. All around were lifelike statues of warriors, of lions, of horses; vases decorated with flowers, birds, dragons; vessels of porcelain, jade and gold.

'Oh wow!' whispered Johnny. 'Isn't this cool?'

'Well cool,' Matt agreed. The only trouble was, they were hardly given time to stop and look at anything. Matt certainly didn't have time to speak to Shawn and see how he was. Mr Pei led them round at a super-brisk pace, calling out the dynasty that each room represented as they walked through, before hurrying on to the next.

'This is great!' said Catarina. 'A museum trip and a speed-walking workout all in one go!' The class laughed.

'Shh!' said Mr Figgis with a warning glance.

'And this is the room of the T'ang Dynasty,' said Mr Pei, 'which ruled China from AD 618 to AD 906 in your Western calendar. Many artefacts of great artistic merit are on display here.'

Matt recognized the room of the T'ang Dynasty: it was the room he'd seen on the virtual tour, the room with the Emperor's Jade Dish. And there it was, a glowing gold and green disc, mounted on its stand in a glass case in the centre of the room. To his surprise, however, Mr Pei did not draw attention to it, but hurried them along, saying, 'Now follow me through to the room of the Five Dynasties – in this period the art of porcelain-making reached new heights –'

'Sorry,' said Matt, 'but – isn't that the Jade Dish over there?'

Mr Pei appeared taken aback for a moment. 'Er, yes, Emperor's Jade Dish, entirely correct. Now let us proceed to the next room, where the porcelain collection is of great interest –'

'But surely we can stop and look at the Jade Dish?' said Matt. 'I mean, isn't that the main reason we're here?' He looked to Mr Figgis.

Mr Figgis cleared his throat. 'We would like to stop and take a proper look, if you don't mind,' he told Mr Pei. 'Our Academy is competing for a replica of that dish in the martial arts tournament next month.'

'Naturally I am aware of that,' said Mr Pei stiffly. 'Very well. There is much to see, but we will make a brief stop here.'

Matt and his friends exchanged puzzled glances. Mr Pei seemed to be behaving strangely – it was almost as if he didn't want them to look at the Jade Dish.

The Tigers Are Formed

Mr Pei led them to the glass case. 'Well, here it is,' he said shortly, and then took a few steps away, as if waiting impatiently for them to finish looking at it and move on.

Everyone clustered around the Jade Dish. 'Don't push!' said Mr Figgis. 'Let everybody have a chance to see.'

The Jade Dish was illuminated from above by a spotlight. Matt gazed at the brilliant golden faces of the dragons, staring out from the rich green background. It was beautiful. The colours were richer, the details more intricate than they had appeared on the computer screen. Apart from that it was just as he remembered – or was it? Looking closer, Matt had a faint sense that something was not right, that there was some subtle difference. But he couldn't put his finger on it. Perhaps he was imagining it? He stared hard at the dish, impressing every detail on his memory.

'Could those at the front step back now – give the others a chance to see!' said Mr Figgis.

Matt stepped back reluctantly. Those who hadn't had a chance to look yet crowded around. Matt looked at a few of the other exhibits while he was waiting – some jade jewellery, some terracotta animals – and he noticed something interesting. The glass cases for these exhibits were slightly dusty and smeary, while the one in which the Jade Dish stood was gleaming. There was also a thin layer of dust covering the floor around the other exhibits – but there hadn't been any dust at all around the case in which the Jade Dish was displayed. *Did the museum pay extra attention to the Jade Dish because it was such a special exhibit?* Matt wondered.

Johnny, meanwhile, was at the front of the little crowd, staring in awe. 'Hey, man, that's beautiful,' Matt heard him say. Johnny turned to Mr Pei. 'I bet you have to be careful cleaning it, don't you? You wouldn't want to drop it!'

There was a murmur of laughter from the

group. Mr Pei, who was still hovering around as if he wanted to get moving, gave a small smile. 'As you say, it is a delicate task. That is why we clean it only once a year. Every Chinese New Year, to be precise.'

Hold on, Matt thought to himself. Chinese New Year was in February. They were in November now. The dish and its case had not been cleaned for nine months if what Mr Pei said was true. But that was not how it looked. Someone had definitely been cleaning up around the case recently. Matt wondered whether to say anything, but Mr Pei didn't give him the chance.

'Now we really must move on,' he said briskly. Clearly, Mr Pei had had enough of the Jade Dish.

'Come along then, class,' said Mr Figgis.

'In the next room,' said Mr Pei, walking rapidly away so that they had to trot to keep up, 'we will see the porcelain of the Five Dynasties, which is remarkable because . . .'

★

'There's something funny going on,' said Matt.
They were back at the Academy. It was after
supper, and he, Shawn, Olivier and Catarina
were in the common room, playing pool.
Johnny was off at basketball practice. The
common room was actually a whole suite
of rooms where pupils could relax outside
lesson-time: there was a room full of the latest
video games, a television room with a huge
widescreen plasma TV, a table-tennis room
with five full-size tables, a quiet room with a
deep-pile carpet and easy chairs and a tropical
aquarium – and there was the pool room. The
pool room overlooked the Academy gardens,
which were landscaped in classical Chinese
style with pagodas, weeping willow trees and
burbling streams crossed by little bridges.

Catarina bent low over the table and lined
up her shot. She struck the cue ball hard; it hit a
yellow ball with a crack and the ball shot across
the table, hitting the corner of a pocket and

bouncing back. She straightened up. 'What do you mean, funny?'

Matt had been thinking about the museum and the Jade Dish. There was something mysterious going on, even though he couldn't put his finger on it. Maybe it had something to do with the break-in? If he could get to the bottom of this, it might shed some light on the unexplained failure of Shawn's dad's security system. Shawn would feel much better knowing what had happened – or might have happened.

'I mean at the museum,' he said. 'Did anyone else notice there was no dust around the Jade Dish? And that the case was cleaner than all the others in that room?'

Shawn shrugged. 'So? They cleaned it up, what about it?'

He took his shot. The red ball just missed the centre pocket. He handed the cue to Olivier.

'But Mr Pei said they only cleaned it at Chinese New Year – why would he say that?

71

Unless someone cleaned it without him knowing?'

'But why would they do that?' asked Shawn.

'That's the mystery!' said Matt.

'I don't get it,' said Catarina. 'So there's no dust, OK. But the Jade Dish is still there, right?'

'Yeah, but what if it's been tampered with in some way? It looked kind of . . . different.'

'I didn't notice that,' said Olivier. 'Why would anyone tamper with it, anyway?'

'I don't know,' said Matt. 'I just think there's something funny going on. Don't forget there was that break-in there a few weeks ago.'

'Yes . . .' said Shawn slowly. 'The way I see it, someone got past my dad's security system that night, and no one has explained how. I reckon it must have been an inside job – someone who knew how the system worked must have disabled it.'

Olivier took his shot, missed and handed the cue to Matt. 'But what's that got to do with the Jade Dish?'

'What if stealing the coins and the postcards was just a cover-up?' said Matt. 'What if there was another cleverer crime that no one knows about? If we could prove there was, and find out who did it –'

'My dad would be in the clear!' said Shawn.

'Right!' said Matt. He bent over the table and took a snap shot; the red ball went racing up the table and dropped into the far pocket.

'Nice!' said Shawn.

'Yeah, but – how're we gonna find out who did it?' asked Catarina. 'Whatever they did.'

'We need to go back to the museum,' said Matt thoughtfully. 'Take a closer look.'

'But it's out of bounds,' objected Olivier. 'We're not allowed to leave school premises without permission.'

'No . . .' said Matt. He had had an idea. It would be far better to visit the museum at night, when it was empty and they could carry on their detective work unobserved. But this would be a very serious breach of school rules indeed. Would the others be up for it?

There was only one way to find out.

'What if we went at night?' he said. 'And broke in?'

There was a short silence. They looked at each other across the table. They had stopped playing now, caught up in the excitement of the idea.

Catarina grinned. 'Hey – sounds like fun! Count me in!'

'If we got caught,' said Olivier, 'we'd be in big trouble.'

'I think it's a great idea,' said Shawn suddenly. 'This business has ruined my dad's reputation. I spoke to him on the phone last night and he's feeling pretty low. I'll take a risk to help him – prove that his security system wasn't at fault.'

'Well, when you put it like that . . .' said Olivier. 'OK – I'm in too. I don't want you guys having all the fun without me!'

'We'll do it tonight!' said Matt. 'We'll go the

museum and find out how anyone could have disabled that system.' Matt knew Shawn had to be right – something dodgy had to be going on. If Shawn's dad was anything like Shawn, he must be a technical genius – there was no way he'd invent a system that simply didn't work. But Matt and his friends would have to operate undercover. 'This has got to be a secret,' he said. 'If anyone finds out what we're doing, we'll probably get expelled.'

'So we don't tell anyone?' said Shawn. 'Not even Johnny?'

Matt thought hard. Johnny was one of his best friends at the Academy. But Johnny was not someone who liked breaking rules. Matt couldn't imagine him breaking into a museum. There would be serious consequences if they got caught. It didn't seem right to risk implicating him, or anyone else. 'No,' he said finally. 'If we're really doing this, we'd better not tell anyone at all. Let's swear each other to secrecy.'

He put out his right hand. The others, forming a circle, did the same and all four hands met.

'We're in this together now,' said Matt.

'A secret society!' said Catarina, laughing. 'Cool!'

'If we're a society,' said Olivier, 'we need a name.'

'Any ideas?' asked Matt, looking around at his friends. No one could think of one.

Matt spied Master Chang through the window. He was walking through the garden, crossing one of the bridges, his head bowed as if deep in thought. The answer dropped straight into Matt's head.

'I've got it!' The others looked at him expectantly. 'Remember Chang's grandfather, and that elite fighting team? We can use their name. The Tangshan Tigers!'

'The Tangshan Tigers!' murmured Shawn.

Catarina and Olivier nodded, smiling. The name was perfect.

The Tangshan Tigers were born.

THE FIRST MISSION

At eleven o'clock that night Matt got out of
bed, taking care not to wake Johnny, who was
snuffling softly in his sleep. He dressed quickly in
dark clothes and slipped out of the room.

The wide landing was lit by a soft blue glow
from panels set into the walls and ceiling. The
same blue glow bathed the stairs. Matt trod
softly, keeping to the shadows as far as he could,
in case any teachers should still be up and about,
or security guards prowling around. But he
didn't see anyone.

Matt was the first to reach the agreed meeting

place: the back entrance, which led to the Academy playing fields. His stomach was tense with excitement. It was a relief when Catarina turned up a minute later, casually chewing gum.

'All right?' whispered Matt.

'No problem.'

Shawn and Olivier arrived together. They all exchanged a thumbs-up, grinning.

'OK,' said Matt. 'Let's go!'

The back door was locked securely, but could be opened from the inside; Matt drew back the bolts and pressed the buzzer to release the catch.

'Wait!' whispered Olivier. 'How are we going to get back in?'

'Good point,' said Matt.

'I know a little trick,' said Catarina. She took her chewing gum and carefully stuck it over the door-catch. 'See?' The door swung to gently behind them, without clicking shut.

'Neat,' said Matt.

The playing fields were silvery-grey in the

moonlight. There was a side-gate that led out on
to the road. As they made their way across the
field towards it Catarina gave a low laugh. 'Wait
a minute! Does anyone remember the way to
the museum?'

'I do,' said Matt. His photographic memory
had recorded the route. Then a thought struck
him. 'It's a long way, though. We'll be out all
night if we walk. Let's take our bikes!'

'Good call,' said Shawn.

The bicycle sheds were on the way to the
gate. Each grabbed his or her bike. Matt was
particularly proud of his bike – a birthday
present from his mum. It was a cool hybrid, with
the chunky wheels of a mountain bike and the
light frame and ten gears of a racing bike. Just
right for speed in the city.

They wheeled their bikes over the field
towards the gate.

'Hold on,' said Matt. 'What are we going to do
about that?'

He pointed at the CCTV camera mounted on top of the gate.

'Let me try something,' said Olivier. He slipped off his jacket and sidled along the perimeter fence towards the camera, keeping out of view. With one deft movement he threw the jacket up in the air. It dropped neatly over the camera and hung there, completely covering the lens.

Shielded from view they unbolted the gate, and a few moments later they were bowling along the road on their bikes. The streets were brightly lit but few cars or people were around. Matt felt the wind blowing through his hair and grinned. They were on their way to solve a mystery *and* prove that Shawn's dad was no dud.

Half an hour later, they had reached the Forbidden City. They came to a stop outside the Palace Museum gates. The gates were secured by a massive, chunky iron padlock.

Matt weighed the lock in his hand. 'No way

are we getting past this! You'd need a chainsaw
to open it.'

'I forgot to bring my chainsaw,' said Catarina.
The others laughed.

'But seriously, what are we going to do?' said
Matt. 'Any ideas?'

'It must be open somewhere,' said Olivier.
'Because look!' He pointed. The windows of the
West Wing were all lit up.

'Let's go round that side, then,' said Matt.

They remounted their bikes and cycled over
there. At closer quarters they could see people
in evening dress, the men in dinner jackets and
the women in glamorous long gowns wandering
back and forth in the yellow rectangles of the
windows.

'Looks like some sort of private viewing,'
said Olivier. 'The opening of an exhibition or
something. I've been to things like this with my
dad before.'

The gate on this side was open. But it was

guarded by two Chinese security men. They stood there stony-faced, arms folded, guns in holsters by their sides.

'Do you think they'll let us in?' said Shawn.

'Leave this to me,' said Olivier.

Olivier's father was a diplomat, and Olivier had grown up accustomed to grand parties and official functions. He had bags of confidence and natural charm. If anyone could blag their way in, it was Olivier. But Matt's heart was beating fast as they approached the guards. What if they thought it strange that four kids should be out so late at night? This was where it could all go wrong.

The guards stared as Olivier walked over.

'Excuse me,' said Olivier with his most winning smile, 'we're so sorry we're late for the party, but we're supposed to meet our parents there. Do you think you could let us through?'

The guards frowned and looked at each other. They moved closer together.

'Ticket,' said one of them.

'Ah, that's the problem, you see,' said Olivier, smiling. 'We were supposed to meet up with our parents earlier and go in with them – they've got the invitations. But we got delayed and missed them. We have got invitations, but they're inside with our parents. So if we could just –'

'Ticket,' repeated the guard.

'Our parents will be waiting inside, you see, and we don't want them to worry. My father is quite an important diplomat, and if you could use your initiative and let us in, I'm sure he'd be grateful –'

'Ticket,' said the guard again.

The Tangshan Tigers glanced at each other.

'Nice chatting with you,' said Catarina.

The gang picked up their bikes, and cycled back to the main entrance. Matt eyed the padlocked gates. They were a good four metres high and ended in a row of nasty-looking spikes. Not much doing there.

'So what do we do?' said Shawn.

What would Chang Sifu do? Matt wondered.

83

He didn't know, but he knew what Chang *wouldn't* do. He wouldn't give up.

'We can't give up before we've started,' said Matt. 'There must be *something* we can do.'

'Yes, but what?'

A shadow fell across the group. They turned slowly to see a young Chinese girl standing in the lamplight. She was about their own age, to judge by her face, but a little smaller. Her eyes were large and dark, and she gazed at the Tangshan Tigers with perfect familiarity, as if she'd been expecting to meet them there.

For a moment nobody spoke.

Then Matt said, 'Hello – can we help you?'

'Perhaps I can help you,' the girl replied in perfect English.

'But who are you?' asked Catarina.

'My name is Li-Lian. I saw you trying to get into the museum. What are you doing here so late?'

Matt hesitated. He didn't want to reveal the gang's secret to anyone, let alone someone they

84

had only just met. 'We're not the only ones up late,' he countered. 'What are you doing here?'

'I live in an apartment nearby. I like to sit up late sometimes, watching the museum in the moonlight. When I saw you trying to get in, I was curious and came out to ask: what are you doing?'

'Well, we've got something important to do,' said Matt cautiously. 'But if we get caught, we'll be in big trouble for doing it. And if you knew about it, you'd be in trouble too. So it's better that you don't know. But we really, really need to get into the museum.'

'It's such a pity that you cannot tell me,' said the girl with a sigh. 'I could help you get inside. But I can't help you get in if I don't know your reason. You might be burglars.'

'We are not burglars –' began Catarina indignantly, but Shawn interrupted.

'She's got a point. Why should she help us break in if she doesn't know why? I vote we tell her.'

'But can we trust her with the secret?' said
Catarina.

'I don't think we have much choice,' said Shawn.

'Anyway, I don't think it matters,' said Olivier.
'We're never going to bump into her again in a
city of ten million people. And she doesn't know
anyone we know.'

Matt came to a decision. 'OK, Li-Lian. This is
a secret, OK?'

The girl nodded gravely. Matt told her about
the theft in the museum, the suspicious failure of
the security system, the cleaned-up display case
and the strange feeling he had about the Jade Dish.
'So we want to get in and do a bit of detective
work,' he concluded. 'Try and pick up some clues.'

Li-Lian's eyes had widened in surprise during
Matt's explanation. Now she gave a grin of pure
pleasure. Obviously, this kind of adventure was
just what she liked most.

'OK,' she said. 'I will get you in. Follow me.'

★

She led them round past the East Wing to the rear of the museum. A section of the railings gave way to a stone wall. It was high, but within arm's length there stood a tree. Matt saw at a glance that it would be possible for them to climb the tree, straddle the wall and let themselves down the other side. It would take nerve, though.

Catarina was the first to go. The tallest and most slender, she was also the best climber. She shinned up the tree, reached across and put her leg over the wall, then dropped down. They heard her land with a thud.

'All right?' called Matt.

'No problem. Come on, you guys!'

Olivier went next, then Shawn. They didn't manage it quite as gracefully as Catarina, but both got over safely. Then it was Matt's turn. He hauled himself up the tree. Soon he was straddling the wall. He looked down at the upturned faces of the Tangshan Tigers. He gulped. It looked a long way down. He had never had a great head for heights . . .

'Come on, Matt!' said Catarina. 'You can do it!'

There was nothing else for it. He took a deep breath. He turned round, gripping the top of the wall.

'Hang down by your arms before you jump,' advised Shawn.

Matt hung by the full length of his arms, letting his legs dangle. His feet must have been about two metres from the ground. Two metres wasn't such a terrible drop . . .

He let go.

He hit the ground hard and staggered. Olivier caught and steadied him.

'All right?' said Shawn.

'I'm fine,' said Matt. He grinned with relief.

He moved back to the railings and waved to Li-Lian. She came towards them.

'Thanks, Li-Lian – we'd have been stuck without you!'

'Yeah, thanks,' said Catarina.

Li-Lian gave a little bow. Her silver hairband glinted in the moonlight. 'It was my pleasure. I wish I could come with you – but I might be missed back at home.'

'You speak very good English,' Matt said. 'Where did you learn it?'

'My grandfather taught me.'

'Your grandfather . . .?' began Matt. But before he could find out any more Shawn said, 'OK – let's get on with it!'

They waved to Li-Lian again and set off towards the museum building. But Matt hung back for a last word – there was something about Li-Lian that intrigued him. He knew he had never met her before, yet there was something familiar about her.

'Why did you trust us? We might have been lying. We might have been burglars like you said.'

Li-Lian smiled. 'I know an honourable soul

89

when I see one. This is something else my grandfather taught me.' She spoke in respectful tones; it was clear that she regarded her grandfather as a great man. 'And now I must go – before someone notices I'm missing!'

She darted across the road. She turned and pointed at a tall apartment block. It stood just behind the walls of the Forbidden City, a huge rectangular building with hundreds of windows. Matt understood that she was telling him where she lived, in case they should ever need her help again.

Matt watched her for a moment.

'Come on!' hissed Shawn.

Matt ran and caught up with the others.

They ran up the broad steps of the museum entrance, and high-fived each other at the top.

'Yes!' said Shawn. 'We're in!'

'Well, nearly,' said Matt. 'But now how do we get past that door?'

'I bet I can get in that window,' said Catarina. She pointed upwards. On the second floor, a tiny window was half open – the gap was too small for an adult, but a girl as slender as Catarina might just wriggle through.

'Do you reckon you could get down to this door and open it within thirty seconds?' asked Shawn.

'No problem!'

'OK,' said Shawn. 'So the alarm's set to go off forty-five seconds after it detects an intruder entering – the idea is to make sure they're well inside before it's activated, so they'll be trapped, right? If you can get me in within thirty seconds, I'll have fifteen seconds to disable it – that should be enough, I hope.'

'Good luck, Catarina!' said Matt.

They waited anxiously as Catarina scaled the wall, making use of a handy drainpipe. She poked her head through the window, turned and gave them a thumbs-up, then, with a squeeze and a wiggle she got her shoulders through. For a second, her long legs remained sticking out of the window. Matt watched her legs kick and, then, with a small cry she slipped completely through the window and her trainers disappeared from sight.

'I hope she's OK,' said Matt.

They waited anxiously.

'*I hope* she can get back down here in less than thirty seconds,' muttered Shawn. 'If I don't disable that alarm in time all hell's gonna break loose. A siren will go off that'll burst your eardrums, all the lights should come on, the security guards' pagers will start bleeping like crazy and an alarm will go off at the local police station!'

Matt counted the seconds ticking away on his watch. Ten. Fifteen. Twenty seconds. Twenty-five . . .

The door burst open, and there stood Catarina, grinning.

Shawn ran past her. He made straight for a

black box mounted on the wall. It displayed a flashing red light. With nimble fingers, Shawn removed the cover and punched in a long series of digits on the keypad.

The red light started flashing faster. Shawn removed the keypad. Underneath was a tangle of wires. Matt watched how carefully he removed one of the wires without touching the others.

'Nearly there,' muttered Shawn. 'Now to disable all the connections.'

The red light was blinking faster. Shawn had only about seven seconds left, Matt calculated.

Beneath the wires was a tiny metal cover. Shawn flipped it open, again without touching any other part of the mechanism, and withdrew a little black silicon chip.

The red light was blinking like mad now. Three seconds.

'Now to make it think it hasn't been disabled,' said Shawn. He deftly, swiftly, inserted another, identical silicon chip he'd produced from

93

somewhere; then plugged in the wire he'd removed.

The red light went out.

The Tangshan Tigers breathed a sigh of relief.

'Way to go, Shawn!' said Matt.

'That was close,' breathed Shawn. 'Within forty-five seconds of the photo-electric cell being broken, you have to key in a sixteen-digit code, remove the keypad, unplug the lead wire and take out the chip. That disables the connections – the guards' pagers and the police alarm and stuff. But then you have to put in a replacement chip and reconnect the lead wire, otherwise the siren will still go off! Do you reckon a bunch of clueless bozos could have done all that?'

'I guess not,' said Olivier.

Quickly, they made their way towards the T'ang Dynasty room. Matt found that he was holding his breath. The museum at night was an eerie place. Statues of lions and bears and Buddhas and warriors watched them in the gloom. They seemed to move around just outside his line of vision, but froze when he looked at them directly. *You're imagining things*, he told himself. *Stop being so jumpy*.

Suddenly he heard a voice. Footsteps clicking on the tiled floor. A light, no, two lights were approaching.

'Quick!' whispered Matt. 'Hide!'

He seized Catarina by the wrist and darted into an alcove. Shawn and Olivier followed, fast. A huge porcelain vase with a pattern of flowers and birds stood in the alcove and they huddled behind it.

Two security guards passed. Matt saw the beams of their torches sweep around the walls, picking out details of the statues and ornaments and paintings. Then gloom settled again. The two men passed on. Their footsteps died away.

Cautiously, the Tangshan Tigers emerged from their hiding place.

'That was *close*!' whispered Catarina.

They moved on. They came to the room of the T'ang Dynasty.

The Emperor's Jade Dish stood in the centre, green and glowing.

They clustered around. Matt looked it over carefully. Then something clicked in his brain.

He gave an involuntary laugh. 'So that's it!'

How could he have missed it? It was like one of those spot-the-difference puzzles he used to do when he was a little kid.

'What?' said Olivier. 'What have you seen?'

'It's these dragons – see those, like, tendrils of hair, or whiskers, or whatever they are, round their faces? In the original, the one I saw on the website, they have three tendrils on each side. But, look, this one only has two.'

Olivier, Shawn and Catarina looked puzzled. Shawn shrugged his shoulders. 'So what does that mean?' he asked.

Matt looked at his friends.

'This dish is a fake!' he told them.

THE OPPONENTS ARRIVE

'Let's take a closer look,' said Shawn. 'The alarm won't go off – the whole system's down now.'

Carefully, he removed the glass case. Olivier reached out and picked up the dish. He hefted it in both hands, looking thoughtful.

'This is not jade,' he announced. 'I've seen and handled plenty of jade – my father collects the stuff. Jade should be heavier than this. This must be, I don't know, toughened glass or something.'

'So what do we do now?' asked Catarina.

'Report it to the museum, of course!' said Shawn. 'They have to know their Jade Dish has

97

been stolen. Then there'll be an investigation – and they'll find out what happened and prove it wasn't my dad's fault!'

'But we can't do that,' Matt objected. 'If we do, we'll have to say how we know. And if Mr Wu discovers that we've sneaked out of bounds at night and broken into the museum, we'll be expelled for sure.'

'And then we can't win the tournament,' said Catarina.

'And we'll have let Master Chang down,' added Matt.

'I tell you what I think,' said Olivier. 'I think we should put the dish back as it was and get out of here while we can. We've got what we came for – now we know for sure it's a fake. Tomorrow we can figure out our next step.'

Olivier moved to put the Jade Dish back on its wooden plinth. 'Wait a minute,' said Matt. 'Look!' He pointed at the plinth – there were some tiny fresh scars on the wood, as though something had been ripped away from it. 'See? The dish must have been glued to the plinth – that's where they pulled it away!'

They replaced the case and retraced their steps towards the back entrance.

They were just turning into the corridor when they were suddenly dazzled by the harsh glare of torches. Matt's heart jumped as though a hand had squeezed it. Behind the glare he made out four dark figures. One of them shouted harshly in Mandarin.

It was the security guards from earlier, plus two others. They marched up and planted themselves in front of the Tigers. Matt felt a sinking sensation in his stomach. They were well and truly caught. They'd be expelled from the Academy for sure – maybe even worse. What would the punishment be for breaking into a museum stuffed with priceless works of art in, of all places, the Forbidden City? For all Matt knew, they might be thrown into prison!

'What are you doing here?' said one of the guards sharply, in English.

Olivier stepped forward, smiling, switching on the charm. 'We're so sorry. We're guests at the reception in the West Wing, and I'm afraid we wandered away. There are so many wonderful exhibits here we couldn't resist coming to take a look. We're really sorry – we didn't mean any harm.'

The faces of the guards relaxed.

'You shouldn't be here,' said one of the guards. 'Our security system should have activated when you came to this part. It has failed again – it is not a good system.'

Matt saw Shawn grit his teeth.

'We'd better get back to our party, then,' said Olivier smoothly. 'We do apologize if we've caused any inconvenience.'

They felt the guards' eyes upon them as they walked away.

'Olivier, that was great,' said Matt in a low

voice. 'You completely saved us back there!'

They passed the alarm and Shawn stopped to replace the chip and reset the system. 'Don't want my dad to get the blame for it not working again!' he said.

From there they made their way to the West Wing. The party was breaking up when they got there. It was easy to join the flow of guests leaving, and to walk out under the noses of the security men who had refused them entry earlier.

They located their bikes and cycled swiftly back to the Academy. Matt saw that Johnny was still fast asleep when he got back to the room. He tumbled into bed, exhausted but elated at his night's work.

As soon as Matt woke up in the morning, he knew what the Tangshan Tigers had to do next.

'OK,' he said to his friends at breakfast in the refectory. 'Here's what we do –' He broke off suddenly. Master Chang was walking past their

101

table. He paused and smiled at Matt and his friends.

'Good morning. Did you sleep well?'

'Er . . . yes, fine thanks, sir,' said Matt.

'You all slept well?'

They nodded.

'I am glad. It is important to rest well before a tournament. No disturbances, then?'

'No, er, no disturbances,' said Matt. Chang nodded and moved away.

'Why was he asking that?' said Catarina. 'You think he's on to us?'

'Maybe he saw us slipping out,' said Olivier.

'Then why didn't he stop us?' asked Shawn.

'But that's just like Chang, isn't it?' said Matt. 'He always has his reasons for what he does, but you can never tell what they are!'

'Anyway,' said Shawn. 'You said you had a plan.'

'Right,' said Matt. 'Let's go back to the museum at lunchtime and ask Mr Pei to show us the dish again. Then we can get him to see that it's a fake for himself.'

'But we won't have time!' objected Olivier. 'If we miss lessons, I think someone will notice.'

'If we skip lunch, we can go there on our bikes and be back in time for afternoon classes at two,' said Matt. 'What do you think?'

'I think,' said Catarina, reaching out for another slice of toast and spreading it thickly with jam, 'if we're going to skip lunch we'd better eat a good breakfast!'

'Yes? What is it?' snapped Mr Pei. He stood at the door of his office, frowning. 'What do you children want?'

'We wondered if you could show us the Emperor's Jade Dish –' began Matt.

'I have already shown it to you.'

'But couldn't we see it again?'

'Nobody is stopping you.'

'But we wanted you to explain it to us, Mr

Pei,' said Olivier. 'Because you're such an expert – you've studied it and you know all the history and everything. You could really teach us a lot!'

'I am a busy man –'

'Oh, please, Mr Pie . . .!' said Catarina.

'My name is Pei, not Pie,' said Mr Pei coldly. Catarina had to clap her hand to her mouth to stifle an attack of the giggles. 'Now go away,' went on Mr Pei. 'Or I will telephone your school to tell them you are here – I suspect without permission.'

He closed the door.

'Well, that's that,' said Shawn dejectedly, as they got on their bikes outside the museum. It looked, Matt thought, much more ordinary, much less creepy than it had done in the moonlight. His thoughts went back to last night, and he remembered Li-Lian and wondered what she was up to right now.

'There's nothing else we can do,' continued Shawn.

'There must be something,' said Matt.

'What would Chang do?' said Catarina suddenly.

They considered this for a moment. 'He wouldn't give up,' said Olivier.

'No, he wouldn't,' said Matt. 'Do you remember, he said if an opponent blocks one move, you must try another.'

'We'll think of something,' said Olivier.

'Come on – race you back to the Academy!' said Catarina, standing up on the pedals of her bike and accelerating away. Matt and the others chased after her, whooping with delight.

Despite the fast ride back to the Academy, they were still late for maths with Miss Barraclough. They crept into the classroom as inconspicuously as they could. Miss Barraclough had set the class some problems and was going around helping pupils individually. Matt liked Miss Barraclough. She was slightly scatty and absent-minded, not like the other teachers. Which was a big advantage now. She was so absorbed in explaining something to a pupil that she didn't look up as Matt and his friends tiptoed across the back of the classroom.

But as they were sitting down Carl called out, 'Hey, where have you guys been? The lesson started twenty minutes ago!' Matt might have known Carl would try and land them in trouble.

Miss Barraclough looked up. 'Yes, you are late. What happened?'

'Er . . .' Matt didn't want to lie. On the other hand the truth wasn't much help either. 'We were, er, studying Chinese culture,' he said hopefully.

'Yeah, right!' scoffed Miles.

Johnny looked at him questioningly. 'What have you been doing?' he whispered. 'More martial arts practice?'

Relieved, Matt nodded. He didn't want to

lie to Johnny – but nodding, he decided, didn't really count as lying.

Mrs Barraclough was still looking at Matt expectantly. 'Studying Chinese culture?' she said. 'Where were you doing that?'

'Er . . .' Matt searched for something to say. He glanced at his friends for help, but no one, not even Olivier, piped up.

They were saved by a tap at the door. Chang Sifu entered. 'Excuse me, Miss Barraclough. May I borrow some squad members you have here? We have important training session this afternoon.'

'Oh yes . . .' said Miss Barraclough. 'I remember Mr Wu said . . . The tournament's very soon, now, isn't it?'

'That is correct. Day after tomorrow.'

'Very well. You'd better take them. And good luck!'

The squad followed Master Chang to the gym. Carl, clearly annoyed at not having landed Matt and his friends in trouble, continued to mutter snide comments about their being late. He was still going on about it when they were changed and standing in the *kwoon*.

'So where were you guys? No one saw you all lunchtime. What were you doing?'

'That is enough, Carl,' said Chang.

'But it's not fair! These guys get to turn up late and no one says a word –'

'Enough,' said Chang more quietly. Carl lapsed into a sulky silence.

'Today,' said Chang, 'we will concentrate on how to control the emotions. He looked pointedly at Carl. 'Do you understand? It is very important to keep emotions under control.'

Carl blushed a furious crimson. Matt noticed that Catarina was biting her lip, trying hard not to laugh.

Chang's gaze turned smoothly to her. 'Very important to control emotions,' he repeated. 'Concentrate on task. In tournament, if before or during your fight you give way to anger – or

laughter – you will lose concentration. What
will happen to you then is quite simple.
Shanghai martial arts team will wipe the floor
with you.' He paused to let this sink in. 'Into
pairs, now. We are going to practise one-handed
block . . .'

The next day, Matt got his first sight of the
Shanghai Academy of Excellence martial arts
team. He was standing in the courtyard with
Shawn when their team bus pulled up. The
tournament wasn't until tomorrow, but the team
had come to see the facilities.

The door of the bus opened and a powerful-
looking middle-aged man, broad-shouldered,
with grizzled hair and a harsh face, was the first
to get off. That must be Sensei Johnson, Matt
guessed. He was followed by a line of eleven
fighters – two girls, nine boys – all dressed in
identical black martial arts outfits. All wore their
hair cut very short, even the girls; all had the same

determined, unsmiling expressions. They formed
into two straight lines behind Sensei Johnson.
There was no laughter, no joking, not even any
conversation between them. Matt felt a jolt in his
stomach – of fear, of excitement, of anticipation.
The tournament seemed more real and closer
than ever before. This time tomorrow he would
be out on the mat fighting for all he was worth
against one of those black-clad warriors.

'Will you look at that?' said Shawn. 'Scary, or
what?'

'They don't look like pushovers, that's for
sure,' said Matt.

The news had spread that the Shanghai team
had arrived, and quite a few of the Beijing
Academy students were coming out of the front
entrance into the courtyard to take a look at
them. Carl came and stood beside Matt and
Shawn.

'That's what I call a martial arts team,' he said.
'See how he's got them drilled? You can bet

your life they don't waste their time playing silly games like we do with Chang.'

'Chang's OK,' said Shawn loyally. 'He knows what he's doing.'

Carl only snorted.

Chang came out and strolled over to greet Sensei Johnson and his team. The two coaches bowed to each other; but Matt saw that even when bowing, Johnson fixed Chang's face with a hostile glare. Chang's expression remained as calm and unruffled as usual.

He and Johnson exchanged a few words – they were a little too far away from Matt to hear what was said – and then Johnson turned and marched towards the school entrance. His team followed, all marching in step like a platoon of soldiers. As they passed, Matt heard Johnson growl to his troops: 'C'mon, team – let's get ready to do some serious damage!'

Chang came over to Matt, Shawn and Carl. 'So you have seen the famous Shanghai team at last.'

'Yes, sir,' said Shawn. 'Where are they going now?'

'To the *kwoon*. I have given them permission to train there today.'

Carl's jaw dropped in disbelief. 'You said – they can train in *our kwoon*? But what about us? Where are we going to train?'

'On playing field,' said Chang mildly. 'Kindly tell all team members to report there in half an hour.'

The sun shone as the team, dressed in their martial arts suits, gathered around Master Chang on the playing field. Trees rustled in the breeze; butterflies flitted through the air.

'Tomorrow, you will face the Shanghai team. As final preparation for this, I have a new training exercise for you.'

Carl sighed heavily. 'Great,' he muttered. 'What is it, hopping about on one leg with our eyes closed, or –'

'It is catching butterflies,' said Chang.

'*What?*' said Carl.

Even Matt, who wanted to side with Chang, couldn't get his head round this one. The whole team looked unconvinced. Olivier looked at Matt and rolled his eyes. Chang didn't seem to notice his team's reaction. He went on calmly, 'There is one more thing. You must catch butterfly without harming it.' He clapped his hands. 'Go.'

Matt spotted a white butterfly just a few metres away and ran for it. Just as he got close, the butterfly abruptly flew in a different direction. Matt followed – he made a jump for it, but again the creature changed course and all he grabbed was a handful of empty air.

All around, his team-mates were chasing, leaping, twisting – and again and again the butterflies fluttered out of reach. The task was much harder than Matt had thought – not only did you need to be observant to spot a butterfly in the first place, you needed energy and stamina to keep running after them, concentration and anticipation to predict where they would fly next, good reactions and suppleness to keep changing direction. After a few minutes of this Matt was breathless and hadn't come near to catching one.

'Hard work, isn't it?' panted Shawn.

'You're telling me!' said Matt. 'Hey, have you had any ideas what to do about the Jade Dish yet?'

Shawn shook his head. 'You?'

'No. I guess we all need to get together and –'

Chang clapped his hands. 'Do not talk! Catch butterflies!'

'Right,' muttered Matt, and made a jump for a yellow butterfly that neatly eluded his grasp.

'Well,' said Chang, calling a halt to the exercise eventually. 'Have you all caught butterflies?'

Panting for breath, they shook their heads – all except Catarina, who grinned proudly. She had her hands cupped together in front of her.

She opened them, and an orange butterfly flew out and spiralled up into the blue sky.

'Excellent, Catarina. You have very good reactions and agility.'

'Yeah, like, really useful for catching butterflies,' said Carl. 'I wish we had Sensei Johnson for a coach – he wouldn't make us waste our time on stuff like this!'

There was a shocked silence. Matt had not seen the point of the training exercise either, but he would never have made a comment like that. It was as rude as it was disloyal.

Chang, however, did not seem to take offence.

'You did not benefit from the exercise then, Carl? Perhaps,' said Chang, 'you will see the point tomorrow.'

Chapter 8

COUNTDOWN TO THE
TOURNAMENT

The day of the tournament dawned.

Matt sat on a bench in the *kwoon*, quietly
trying to focus on the challenge that lay ahead.
But it was difficult to stay calm. He turned to
Shawn, who was sitting beside him.

'This is it then,' he said. 'Here we are.'

'Yeah,' Shawn agreed, moistening his lips. 'Funny
to think in an hour and a half it'll all be over.'

On the other side, the Shanghai team, clothed
in their ominous black, stared across at them,
trying to psych them out.

The head judge, Mr Lau, took his place at the judges' table. The assistant judges brought in the Emperor's Jade Dish and placed it in the middle of the table, balanced on a stand. The dish! Matt stared at it from across the room. He had to find out if the dish on the stand was the original.

Pretending he needed to stretch his legs, he strolled over to take a closer look.

On this dish, Matt saw, the dragon had three locks of hair framing each side of its face – just as the original did! Still, it might just be an exact replica. He walked behind the judges' table and sneaked a look at the back. What he saw made his heart leap with excitement. There were tiny splinters of wood stuck to the back of the Jade Dish. That must be where it had been ripped away from its plinth in the museum!

He made his way back to the team. He tried not to walk too quickly. In a low voice, he said to the other Tigers: 'That's the original. There's been a swap!'

'How do you know?' asked Shawn, looking over at the dish.

'There are splinters of wood sticking to it – you can see where it was stuck to the plinth!'

'I don't get it,' said Catarina. 'Why swap them?'

'I don't know,' said Matt. 'But the question is, what do we do?'

'Should we tell the judges?' suggested Olivier.

'Not just before the tournament!' Matt said. 'Besides, the only proof we've got is the splinters and we're not supposed to know about that, are we?'

The *kwoon* was beginning to fill up. Seats were placed on three sides of the *tatami* mat – the judges' table stood on the fourth – and spectators were arriving every moment and sitting down. He saw Johnny take his seat on the other side of the hall. Johnny caught his eye, mimed a karate chop and mouthed 'Good luck!'

Matt kept a look out for his mother. Meanwhile, he noticed Mr Pei from the museum arrive. Mr Pei went over to Sensei Johnson and soon the two were deep in conversation.

'What's Mr Pei doing here?' Matt muttered to himself. Chang was standing close by and answered: 'Mr Pei is here to present the award, since it is based on a piece in the museum's collection.'

'But why's he talking to Sensei Johnson?' Matt asked.

'Ah,' said Chang. 'Something to do with the presentation ceremony? Or some other issue of concern to them both? Who knows?'

Matt watched Sensei Johnson and Mr Pei carefully. They were talking heatedly now, Johnson chopping the air with his hand as though insisting on something, Mr Pei arguing back furiously. *What was that all about?* Matt wondered. As he watched, Mr Pei and Sensei Johnson seemed to suddenly remember that they were in a public place. They both gave forced, polite smiles and drew apart.

Mr Lau cleared his throat and announced, 'Ladies and gentlemen – the tournament will commence in fifteen minutes.'

Matt's head was buzzing. He needed to talk with the other Tangshan Tigers – right now. They knew the real dish had been stolen and was sitting right there on the judges' table – but how could they prove it without incriminating themselves?

Matt felt as though his head was about to explode when he heard the calm, measured tones of Master Chang addressing the team.

'It is time to ready ourselves. Everybody stand. Relax, drop shoulders. Breathe slowly in, out, in, out. You are sleeping tigers. Soon tiger will awake, but not yet. Now, it rests.'

Matt let his shoulders drop. He felt his sinews relax as he breathed deeply in and out. His mind was clearing.

'Soon it will be time,' said Chang. 'And remember – pace yourselves. Do not rush into anything.' He gave Matt a long look, and Matt wondered what he meant exactly. Was Chang talking about the tournament – or something else?

'Let us warm up,' said Chang.

He began to put the team through a routine of warm-up exercises, starting gently with neck rotations. On the opposite side of the mat, Sensei Johnson was putting his team through a more strenuous routine, involving violent punching and shouting.

An idea came to Matt.

'Master Chang?' he said. 'Could I go to the changing room, just for a few minutes? With Shawn and Olivier and Catarina?'

Chang Sifu looked at him. 'Why?'

'Well, we've been practising some moves – you know we train together – and we want to run through them one more time. Because we want to use them in the tournament. But we can't let the Shanghai team see, otherwise they'll know what to expect.'

'I see,' said Chang thoughtfully. 'And they are important to you, these . . . moves?'

'They're very important, sir,' said Shawn.

'Very well,' said Chang. 'Five minutes.'

'Hey, how come you're letting those guys slope away?' protested Carl loudly.

'Because I trust them,' Matt heard Chang say, as he led the Tangshan Tigers to the changing room.

'OK,' said Matt, 'this is the problem. We know that Jade Dish is the real one, stolen from the museum. But how can we prove that without giving it away that we broke in?'

'There's another problem too,' said Shawn. 'We need to prove that the theft was an inside job, that my dad's security system didn't fail.'

'We have to expose the culprits,' said Olivier. 'It's no good just saying, "Oh, look, here's the original dish, I wonder how that got here."'

'And how did it get there, anyway?' asked Shawn.

'We need to think,' said Matt. The changing room had an interactive whiteboard, which Chang occasionally used to illustrate team tactics. Matt drew a large circle on it with a cartoon dragon's head in the middle. 'That's the Jade Dish, right? Here –' he wrote 'Mr P' in one corner – 'is Mr Pei, and here –' he wrote 'SJ' in the opposite corner – 'is Sensei Johnson. Now, what's the connection?'

'The Jade Dish was in Mr Pei's museum,' said Shawn at once.

'Right,' said Matt. He drew an arrow from Mr P to the dish. 'And what about Johnson?'

'He was expecting to win the dish!' said Catarina.

'Right!' said Matt again – and he drew an arrow from the Jade Dish to SJ. 'Now we also saw Mr Pei and Johnson talking together today, like they know each other – so there's

a connection between them too!' He drew
a double-headed arrow connecting the two
names. 'So the dish was going to go from Pei to
Johnson, that was the plan –'

'But that would have taken months of
planning!' said Olivier. 'They'd have to arrange
the theft, disable the security system, and make
sure to coincide with the tournament!'

'They've had months,' said Matt. 'The date
of this tournament was fixed well in advance.
I'd guess either Mr Pei, approached Johnson, or
Johnson approached Mr Pei, and they cooked it
up between them to smuggle out the real dish
and present it to the winners – then they'd sell it
and split the proceeds!'

'But how could they be sure the Shanghai
Academy would win?' asked Catarina.

'Over-confidence, I guess,' said Matt. 'They'd
won it six years in a row, so it must have seemed
like a good bet.'

Olivier gave a low whistle. 'It's a pretty clever

way to steal a valuable art treasure, you have to
admit. To have it awarded to you in public with
everyone clapping!'

'That's it!' said Catarina. 'I never trusted that
Mr Pie!'

'The only problem is, we don't have any
evidence!' said Shawn. 'How are we going to
prove it?'

'The only way I can see,' said Matt, 'is that we
have to win the tournament! Then we'll have the
Jade Dish – and we can somehow "discover" it's
the real one – and find a way to prove who stole
it! But the first thing is to win, right? Because, if
we don't win, the Jade Dish goes home with the
Shanghai team and we never see it again.'

'Right,' said Catarina. 'So let's go out there
and win!'

Chapter 9

COMBAT!

'Ah – you are ready?' said Chang Sifu, as Matt and the Tangshan Tigers returned to the team bench. 'You have perfected your – moves?'

'I think so,' said Matt. 'We know what we've got to do!'

'Good,' said Chang. 'I have here running order for the tournament. You will be fighting last, Matt – against the Shanghai captain, Anthony Brooke.'

A thrill of anticipation ran through Matt – partly nerves, partly excitement. He knew the name. Brooke had quite a reputation. He had never lost a competitive fight. He was a *karateka*, also expert in ju–jitsu. He was said to be the dirtiest fighter in the Shanghai team. And that was saying something.

It was quite an honour to be pitted against the Shanghai captain. Matt was determined to acquit himself well. It was possible, of course, that by the time the last bout was fought, Beijing would already have an unassailable lead; but it was equally possible that the match would go to the wire, and then, Matt realized, he would have to fight with everything he had.

He looked across at the Shanghai team, wondering which one was Brooke. At that moment, one of the Shanghai fighters detached himself from the group and walked over to the Beijing team. He was tall and muscular and walked with a confident swagger. He had dark hair and pale blue eyes that seemed to stare right through the Beijing team. Matt thought he was a seriously tough-looking individual.

'Hi, I'm Anthony Brooke,' he said, smiling. Matt noticed the way that the smile didn't reach his pale blue eyes. 'I just came to say: good luck.'

'Thanks,' said Matt, thinking someone should speak up on behalf of the Beijing team. 'You too.'

'We won't need luck,' said Brooke, still smiling. 'But you will. You'll need a miracle.'

Before anyone could reply, Brooke had turned his back on them and was swaggering with deliberate, provocative slowness back to his team.

'Take no notice,' said Chang quietly. 'He is trying to anger you. Remember importance of controlling emotions.'

Only a minute to go now. The hall was full. Matt saw Mr Wu, dressed with impeccable smartness as usual, sitting in the centre of the front row. His face was calm, but the way he twisted his fingers together in his lap showed the tension he was feeling. Then Matt saw his mother. She smiled and waved at him. Matt felt his face flush with pleasure.

Mr Lau struck a tiny silver bell on the table in front of him. 'The tournament will begin. Bout One: Wolfgang Becker of the Beijing International Academy versus Ricky Lopez of the Shanghai Academy of Excellence.'

Chang touched Wolfgang on the shoulder. 'Remember what you have learned.'

The first bout began.

It was a fast and furious fight. Matt saw at once that the Shanghai team intended to take no prisoners. The Shanghai fighter, a judo specialist like Wolfgang, attacked relentlessly, but Wolfgang defended well and was able to hold his own – until Sensei Johnson, from the side, barked out a command. In response, the Shanghai fighter whipped in a punch that started low, travelled up and struck Wolfgang in the eye. Matt cried out in protest. A shout went up from all the Beijing supporters. It was a strict rule that no blows to the neck or head were permitted. But the punch had been cleverly thrown on the blind side of the judges; they had not seen it and could not give a foul. Half-blinded, Wolfgang could no longer defend himself. The Shanghai fighter got him in a ju-jitsu armlock, forced him down on the mat and held him there.

One—nil to Shanghai.

A bad start. Matt couldn't believe it.

And it got worse. In the next bout, no illegal blows were used, but the Beijing fighter – a Lebanese boy named Abdul – was constantly wary of the possibility and this made him lack confidence. The Shanghai fighter was hot stuff, Matt had to concede, and he floored Abdul with a flurry of kicks and punches right in front of the judges' table.

Two—nil to Shanghai.

And Beijing needed to win six out of nine, Matt realized.

The noise level in the hall was rising. Some of the spectators were getting to their feet, calling out, 'Come on, Beijing!' and 'Come on, Shanghai!'

Although it was a home match for the Beijing
International Academy, the Shanghai Academy of
Excellence had brought a lot of fans with them.

In the midst of all the noise, Chang remained
calm and impassive. He touched Catarina's
shoulder. 'Remember what you have learned.'

'Watch out for your face,' said Matt.

'She hits my face, she's gonna wish she hadn't!'
was all Catarina said. She walked out to fight.
Gracefully dancing round her opponent, easily
avoiding or blocking the girl's attacks, she built
up a clear lead, landing several kicks to the body.
Sensei Johnson barked out his order again as
soon as Catarina had her back to the judges'
table. But Catarina was ready for that one. As the
girl struck at her face Catarina grabbed her wrist
and in one easy movement threw her flat on her
back. Matt jumped to his feet.

'Go, Catarina!' he called out. The Beijing
team cheered wildly.

Two–one.

Carl Warrick was up next. 'Remember what you have learned,' said Chang.

'Yeah, right,' said Carl, with a curl of the lip. He swaggered out on to the mat.

His opponent was a tall, shaven-headed, tough-looking boy of Asian appearance. They gave each other a bow that was little more than a nod.

As soon as the bout began, Carl rushed to the attack, launching a combination of strikes and kicks. His opponent blocked them all, hard. Then he counter-attacked. He was a kung fu exponent, fast and agile. Carl was soon reeling before an onslaught of body–punches and high kicks. Matt couldn't help feeling sorry for him – he was outclassed and had no answer to the other's fighting style. But whatever Carl's faults he did not lack courage. He hung in as best he could, and stayed on his feet. He was able to avoid some of the more vicious strikes, the ones aimed at the face or neck, by twisting away, shifting his centre of gravity, constantly changing direction. Matt

was reminded of something, and then he got it
– Carl's evasive action was exactly like the agile,
twisting movements they had performed when
trying to catch the butterflies. It was this that
saved him from more serious punishment.

The bout ended. The verdict was never in
doubt.

Three–one to Shanghai.

And now Beijing needed to win five out of
seven.

Carl came back to his team area looking shell-
shocked. 'Sorry,' he mumbled.

'No need to feel sorry,' Chang told him
swiftly. 'Today you met a stronger fighter. You
fought with spirit.'

Carl didn't answer, but sat down and studied
the floor.

Next up was Shawn.

'Good luck!' said Matt, clapping his friend on
the shoulder..

Shawn fought cautiously at first. The Shanghai

fighter, a ju-jitsu specialist, kept trying to get him off balance and take him down on the mat. But Shawn kept his balance superbly – and at last he saw his moment and swept the Shanghai fighter off his feet with a *ko soto gari* throw. He pinned him on the mat with a scarf hold.

Three–two!

Shawn returned to the team area smiling.

'Way to go, Shawn!' said Matt, delighted both for his friend and for the team.

'It was all that work on balance we did with Chang!'

Things were looking up for the Beijing team. Olivier, and the Italian boy, Dani, both won the next two bouts for Beijing, benefiting from Chang's training in observation. They watched their opponents like hawks, protecting themselves against illegal blows, anticipating attacks and spotting the precise moment to counter-attack.

Four–three to Beijing!

Sensei Johnson was red in the face now, pumped up, shouting and roaring at his team. And Mr Pei, Matt noticed, was feeling the strain. His face wore a hunted look, and he was biting his lip.

But, urged on by Johnson's frantic shouting, Shanghai won the next bout, their fighter landing another illegal blow on the blind side of the judges.

Four–all.

Then Beijing scored another victory. Lola, the daughter of a Nigerian businessman and the only other girl in the team apart from Catarina, made it five–four.

Shanghai came storming back and won the next.

Five–all!

Everything hinged on Matt's final bout. The winner of this would deliver a six–five victory to their whole team.

'Matt James and Anthony Brooke,' called the head judge.

'Remember what you have learned,' said Chang quietly.

It seemed a long way to the centre of the *tatami*. Matt blanked out the noise of the excited spectators; he blanked out everything except the fight ahead of him. The world had shrunk to himself, his opponent and the *tatami* mat they were fighting on.

Matt stood facing Anthony Brooke. The two boys locked gazes.

'Matt, huh?' says Brooke softly. 'That's where I'm gonna put you, kid. On the mat!'

'You're welcome to try.'

They bowed.

The bout began.

They circled one another warily. Brooke came in with a spear-hand thrust at the body. Matt blocked this double-handed, but he sensed it wasn't a serious attack, just a testing of his defences. He didn't counter-attack immediately.

He was watching, observing, as Chang had taught him to do.

Brooke came forward again. He aimed a karate chop at the side of Matt's neck – a seriously illegal blow, which could have put Matt in hospital if it had connected – but it didn't connect. Matt dodged in the nick of time. And he had spotted something. Brooke had a trick of feinting by dropping his left shoulder, so that you thought he was going to strike from that side, then attacking with the right hand instead. But there was no time to dwell on this. Brooke launched a front kick at his stomach! Matt stopped it with a downward block and now, for the first time, he counter-attacked, landing a kick squarely in Brooke's ribs. Thud! That felt good. Brooke backed off.

Matt, emboldened, went on to the attack with another kick, a sweeping crescent kick, which Brooke blocked at waist height. Sensing he had Brooke on the retreat Matt tried a forward punch straight through Brooke's guard – but that was too obvious, a terrible mistake. *No!* thought Matt as Brooke blocked, grabbed his arm and swivelled. Now Matt was caught in an armlock. Brooke tightened the lock – the pain was excruciating; it felt as if Brooke was trying to break his arm. But Matt still had the other arm free. He delivered two short, fast punches to Brooke's side, as Chang had taught him. Brooke grunted, his grip loosened momentarily and Matt pulled free.

Brooke came straight after him, throwing punches and chops at Matt's face and neck, illegal attacks that Matt only just avoided. Brooke was not even on the blind side of the judges; he didn't seem to care any more – he was desperate to win at all costs even if he got disqualified afterwards. Matt just wanted to avoid serious injury. He stayed calm, controlling his emotions as Chang had taught him. He dodged. He blocked. He watched. And then he saw it

– that drop of the left shoulder. Matt knew what was coming next. When Brooke moved to strike with the right hand his defence would be momentarily down. Matt had a quarter of a second in which to act.

And he used it.

He turned, he twisted and he executed a back kick with all the speed and force he possessed. Brooke ran straight into it. Matt felt his heel driving hard into Brooke's midriff, all the strength of his body behind it.

Brooke crashed back on to the mat. He didn't get up. He could hardly breathe.

It was over. The fight was over.

Matt was the winner.

The world around him swam back into focus. Matt heard the cheering, he saw his mother standing up to clap, he saw his team-mates jumping around wildly. Even Chang was smiling.

Beijing International Academy six; Shanghai Academy of Excellence five.

For the first time in six years, the trophy was coming back to Beijing.

'It gives me great pleasure,' said Mr Wu, and Matt could see that he meant it – he was smiling all over his face, 'to present this fine replica of the Emperor's Jade Dish to the Beijing International Academy!'

Chang Sifu gave Matt a tap on the shoulder and nodded; it was for him, as winner of the final bout, to go up and collect the trophy.

Matt's head was spinning as he walked towards the judges' table. What should he do next? Just accept the Jade Dish and then later reveal that it was genuine and confide his suspicions of Sensei Johnson and Mr Pei to Chang Sifu? There didn't seem much else he could do, but he was troubled that he didn't have the definite proof that they needed to put Shawn's dad in the clear . . .

★

He held the beautiful trophy aloft. The Beijing supporters' cheers rang up to the ceiling. He saw Johnny grinning, his mother clapping for all she was worth. Mr Pei stood on the podium by the judges' table, looking as sour as if he'd just bitten into a lemon.

And suddenly Matt's mind went into overdrive!

This was too good an opportunity to miss.

As the cheering died down, Matt made a show of examining the Jade Dish closely.

'Er, I think there's something a bit funny here,' he said. 'Something a bit funny about this dish.'

A hush fell.

'What do you mean?' said Mr Wu, his smile fading.

'It's really heavy, like it's made of real jade or something. And there are these weird bits of wood stuck to the back of it – as if it used to be glued to a plinth. I might be wrong, but . . . are we sure this is a replica? It couldn't be the original, could it?'

Mr Pei was looking ill now.

'What do you mean?' said Mr Wu again. 'Of course it is a replica. Let me see —'

'If we had an art expert here — but wait a minute!' said Matt. 'We do have an art expert! Mr Pei, what do you think?'

He placed the Jade Dish on the table in front of Mr Pei.

Matt heard Olivier give a low whistle, and Catarina laughed. They had both seen the trap Matt had laid for Mr Pei. Mr Wu and the other judges were looking closely at the dish now. Mr Pei could hardly deny the Jade Dish was genuine — if he did, and it was shown to be real, everyone would know he had lied. On the other hand, if he admitted it was the real thing, the game was up: there'd be no chance of winning it back at next year's tournament, or ever again. It would be returned to the museum, placed under heightened security, and his own role in its disappearance would be

investigated. There was nothing he could do
– no way out.

Mr Pei looked helplessly at the dish, then at
Sensei Johnson.

'I–I,' he stammered. 'I don't –'

'What's the problem?' said Johnson. 'Is it
genuine or not?'

'But . . . you . . .'

'Hey, don't look at me,' said Johnson. 'I'm not
the art expert – you are!'

Matt was puzzled. Johnson looked and
sounded innocent, compared to the guilty,
stuttering Mr Pei. Could it be that Johnson had
had nothing to do with it? Had he been talking
to Mr Pei about something else?

Mr Pei looked wildly around, like a hunted
rabbit. Then, abruptly, he jumped down from
the podium and ran for the door.

'After him!' shouted Sensei Johnson. 'He's a
thief!'

There was a buzz of consternation. Everyone

moved towards the door and several people ran out after Mr Pei.

Mr Wu strode towards the door, taking out his mobile. 'Security? Do not allow Mr Pei to leave the building. And call the police immediately!'

All eyes were fixed on the end of the hall where Mr Pei had escaped. It was a surprise for Matt when he turned back to the judges' table and saw that the Jade Dish had gone.

So had Sensei Johnson.

'Which way?' said Catarina.

'Where can they go?' asked Olivier. 'All the exits are being sealed.'

'Unless . . .' Matt had an idea. He looked up and noticed Chang stood outside the doorway of the dorm, watching. He blinked once, slowly, and Matt felt as though his teacher was waiting to see what he would do next. 'They won't get past the security guards at the entrance, but what about the car park? Johnson's school bus is there – and the exit is automatic if you've got a visitor's pass, isn't it?'

Shawn nodded. 'You're right. It's probably the only way they can still get out – let's go!'

The car park was a large underground space lit by bright white lights with glittering steel pillars.

'There he is!' said Matt. Sensei Johnson was just getting into the school bus, holding the Jade Dish under his arm.

He turned and saw them. A scowl distorted his face.

'Stay back, kids – I'm warning you. I'm getting outta here – and no one's going to stop me!'

'Are you sure of that?' said Olivier.

The Tangshan Tigers slowly approached.

'Why don't you put the dish down?' said Matt. 'You don't want it to get broken.'

'The only thing that's gonna get broken, kid,' said Johnson, 'is your neck!'

He swiped viciously at Matt with the dish. Matt

ducked, feeling the wind from the blow ruffle his hair. He launched himself forward and flung his arms round Johnson's knees, making him stagger.

Johnson raised his hand to bring a karate chop down on Matt's neck, but Olivier darted forward and blocked the blow. He and Shawn hung on to Johnson's arms, preventing him from striking.

'Let me go!'

'Not likely!' said Catarina.

'Let go – or I'll drop the dish. It won't be so priceless when it's in a thousand pieces!'

'You wouldn't!' said Olivier.

'Wouldn't I?'

Sensei Johnson released the dish.

Matt saw it plunging towards the concrete floor of the car park, twisting, turning, flashing gold and emerald under the bright lights – and then he saw Catarina diving gracefully forward, catching it with two outstretched hands a centimetre above the floor.

Johnson struggled even harder. He was a powerful man and managed to break free.

'Give me that dish, girl!' he hissed.

'No,' said Catarina. She was on her feet now, holding the dish protectively. 'You won't look after it.'

Johnson charged at Catarina – but Matt, Shawn and Olivier barred his way. He aimed a volley of kicks and punches at them – but the Tangshan Tigers, well trained by Chang, dodged and blocked expertly. Catarina carefully placed the Jade Dish behind a pillar and helped the others defend themselves against Johnson's assault. Johnson was a trained and powerful athlete, and could certainly have beaten one or two, perhaps even three Tangshan Tigers. But four were too much for him.

Matt blocked a karate chop double handed; Shawn grabbed Johnson's other arm and pulled; Catarina stuck out a long leg so that he stumbled over it; Olivier gave him the final push that sent him face first to the ground.

Oliver sat on his legs; Matt and Shawn took an arm each.

In the distance, they heard the sound of a police siren.

'Do you want to go and tell them where we are, Catarina?' said Matt.

'Sure thing. Don't go anywhere, will you?'

'Don't worry,' said Matt. 'We won't.'

The police led Johnson to the foyer. The Tangshan Tigers went with them. Mr Pei had already been caught and was standing between two police officers. He looked at Johnson balefully.

'I never should have listened to you!' said Mr Pei. 'It was a crazy plan; I told you from the start!'

'Yeah? Well, you were happy enough to come in for a share of the profits, weren't you?'

'I am arresting you both and you will be charged with theft,' said the police inspector. 'You do not have to say anything, but I should warn you that anything you do say may be taken down and used in evidence –'

'All right!' screamed Johnson. 'I did it! I tried to steal something that would have kept me in comfort for the rest of my life! Do you blame me? I'm getting old; I won't be able to coach for much longer – I need to support myself when I retire. You were happy enough to come in on it for a share of the loot, Pei. Everyone's in it for the money, aren't they? Everyone's corruptible!'

But they're not, thought Matt. He exchanged glances with the Tangshan Tigers and saw they were all thinking the same thing. Chang Sifu wasn't corruptible. No amount of money would ever make him do anything dishonourable.

'Take them away,' said the inspector.

Later that day, the journalists arrived. They turned up at the school gates in a pack, toting notebooks and cameras and recording devices.

Matt and his friends were watching through the window.

'Hey, we're big news!' said Catarina.

'It's fantastic!' said Shawn. 'Those same journalists who made fun of my dad – now they're going to have to eat their words. They'll have to explain that there's nothing wrong with my dad's security system, except that Mr Pei switched it off.'

'And it's all thanks to us!' said Matt. 'The Tangshan Tigers! We won our first tournament and we cracked our first case!'

'High fives!' said Catarina – and they all high-fived each other, laughing in delight.

'Yes, you are right to celebrate,' said a voice. It was Master Chang, who had entered the room without anyone noticing. He could move as quietly as a cat when he wanted to. 'You deserve your celebration.'

'Oh, you mean . . . for winning the tournament?' said Matt. He wasn't sure how much Chang had heard.

The ghost of a smile hovered on Chang's lips. 'Yes, that too,' he said. 'I wish you luck with the next one.'

'The next tournament?'

'Yes,' said Chang softly. 'That too.'

As Chang left the room, Matt and his friends looked at each other. 'What do you think he meant?' Matt asked. Catarina laughed.

'Who knows?' she said. 'Chang Sifu is a mystery.' The others laughed too, then turned to look out of the window at the crowd of reporters. All of this was because the Tangshan Tigers had solved their first mystery.

'I wonder what the Tangshan Tigers will do next,' Olivier said.

Matt smiled. 'Who knows?' he said. 'But I can tell you one thing.' His friends waited to hear what he would say next. 'I've got a feeling it's going to be a great adventure!'

Matt

Masters of Martial Arts
Fighters of Crime
together they're the

TANGSHAN TIGERS

Shawn

Catarina

puffin.co.uk

Olivier

TANGSHAN TIGERS

Matt James

Age: 12

Nationality: British

Sport: Tae kwon-do

Special skill: Photographic memory

Strengths: Being flexible and picking up techniques from other martial arts.

As a crime fighter, he is a natural leader of the Tangshan Tigers.

Weaknesses: Sometimes too keen to jump into a mystery without careful planning.

Join the Team and Win a Prize!

Do YOU have what it takes to be a Tangshan Tiger?

Answer the questions below for the chance to win an exclusive Tangshan Tigers kit bag. Kit bag contains T-shirt, headband and cloth badge.*

1. What is the Chinese term for 'training hall'?
   a) *Kwoon*   **b)** *Karateka*   **c)** *Kufu*

2. Catarina's specialty is capoeira. Which country does this martial art come from?
   a) Britain   **b)** Bolivia   **c)** Brazil

3. In Karate, a sequence of movements performed without a partner is called *kata*.
   a) True   **b)** False

Send your answers in to us with your name, date of birth and address. Each month we will put every correct answer in a draw and pick out one lucky winner.

Tangshan Tigers Competition, Puffin Marketing, 80 Strand, London WC2R 0RL

Closing date is 31 August 2010.